A.I. ZOMBIE

L.A. JOHNSON

CHEMICAL ZOMBIE PRESS

This book is a work of fiction. The names, characters and events in this book are the products of the author's imagination or are used fictitiously. Any similarity to real persons living or dead is coincidental and not intended by the author.

Published by Chemical Zombie Press LLC

Cover Artwork by Christian Kallias
Editing by Elizabeth Lance

1

Lyra looked around the waiting room at the lime green walls and sighed. Who in their right mind had let a jellyfish choose the paint color? The jellyfish in question, Gorb, was busy at the moment manning the hospital check-in desk. She was trying to sneak up on him.

Her phone buzzed a notification. She muted the phone and looked around, but Gorb didn't seem to have noticed. Whew.

She glanced down at the phone to see what the notification was. It was Ian, reminding her again about her guest appearance on his popular web show, Fear Zone Universe. She put the phone away.

When she looked up, Gorb was distracted by a new arrival. Yes! Panther-like- no wait, ninja-like, she snuck up behind the desk and snatched the full, steaming, cup of coffee with sugar and cream. Then she tiptoed across the room and around the corner.

"Hey!" Gorb yelled. "My coffee's gone. I know it was you, Lyra!"

"Thanks, Gorb," she called out.

“Fine,” she heard him mutter, “I’ll go get some more.”

Lyra smiled and continued down the hall. That’s when she saw Arthur trying to make eye contact with her and attempted to hurry past.

Arthur just followed and raised an eyebrow. "I have to admit, Lyra, you are top notch, both as a doctor and as a person."

"Stop kissing up, Arthur, it's not going to make your life any easier."

"No, that's not what I meant," he said, stepping in her way.

She tried to look at him as murderously as possible, but somehow it wasn't getting through. "Don't think my Hippocratic Oath won't keep me from hurting you," she said.

He stepped aside but, unfortunately, continued, "What I mean is, why in stars name are you way out here in the middle of nowhere if you're actually competent?"

"Look," she said, holding him against the wall. "One, watch your language when we're in patient areas of the hospital. Two, I realize that you're fairly new here and that you're really annoying, but every doctor, nurse, and clerk here are all first rate. And frankly, they're all better than you. We happen to be the best at what we do. And three, well, just go ahead and say it."

He tried to wriggle free, but she held him there.

"Say. It."

“Under the coat,” he said, “all your leather and tattoos that everybody can see, well I think it’s holding your career back. As a doctor. And trust me, you’re gorgeous and all-” His face turned red.

“Careful,” Lyra said and narrowed her eyes at him. Arthur wasn’t bad himself. He was tall with sandy brown hair and thoughtful eyes.

“Well,” he bravely continued, “I’m just afraid nobody will take you seriously.”

He was right, though, a little. On a normal planet, it would be a problem. It was one of the reasons why she was on a space station at the edge of the universe and not on a normal planet. “I like myself, Arthur,” she said. “You should try it sometime. Besides, everybody here takes me seriously. Just wait until the first thing goes wrong, you’ll see.” She raised an eyebrow at him. “There’s more? Fine, out with it, then.”

"Why are you out here next to an unstable black hole on purpose?" he blurted out.

"And there it is," she said, releasing him. "You're a scaredy-cat as well as a marginal doctor."

"Resident," he said. "And I won't be here long, I've put in transfer papers to a dozen systems. When I get back to my home-world, I will put in a good word for you. We have a beautiful planet, excellent benefits, the best laboratories-"

"Not interested," she said, jetting past him down the hallway and not slowing down to see if he was even there to listen to what she was saying as she continued. "And what in the galaxy's back end would make you think that I need job offers from idiot interns?"

"You said to watch our language in the patient areas," he reminded, not as far behind her as she had hoped. She stopped and turned to him.

"I told you to watch your language. Because I'm in charge. And you're a peon. I can say whatever I want wherever I want."

Another doctor walked by and smirked. She was interested in what was going on, but obviously too smart to stop. She waved at them.

"Hi, Emily. Good morning." Lyra said.

"Why are you nice to her?" Arthur asked.

"She's earned it. You haven't. And now you have set yourself back even further. If you keep this up, you'll be retired before I'm nice to you again."

"I don't know if you didn't hear me or if you just aren't listening," he persisted, "but I'm not going to be here very long."

"I heard you," she said. "Now, you listen to me, this small

hospital serves this entire space station and the dozen or so surrounding planets. If we weren't shorthanded, you'd be gone already."

She kept going and even though she didn't look back, she could tell he had fallen behind this time. Good riddance.

The one thing she couldn't stomach was short-timers. Because what they didn't get was that everybody here was here on purpose, not out of necessity or obligation. And that's what made this place work. Rule number one, to Lyra, was that everything and everybody could be fixed with one tiny caveat, they had to want to be here on Celestica.

Lyra's phone buzzed. This time it was a notification from Gorb that she had a new patient. She put the phone down and walked down the hallway to meet the gurney.

"Hello, I'm Lyra. You're going to be okay, Mr...." She looked around for notes and didn't find any, so she raised her voice so that anybody in the vicinity who had the information could answer. After all, Gorb had a habit of lurking nearby. "What have we got, people? Is he a resident, a tourist, or an evil administrator?" She winked at the young patient.

The patient looked up at her wide-eyed and muttered, "Blackhole." His face contorted in fear.

Lyra shook her head. Tourist.

"You're perfectly safe here. Celestica Space Station is an absolutely stable distance from the black hole, ok?"

She could tell by his face that she wasn't getting through.

Okay, I'll try again. "Look, unless you're immortal or something, your lifespan is a good eighty to one hundred and twenty years, right?"

He nodded, his face still a mask of worry.

"If you showed up here thinking you're risking death by black hole, then, you're approximately three hundred and eighty billion years early. Now, we can fix up that wound and then you can go home with no issues other than a very cool scar and a story for your friends about how you went to Celestica Space Station and got stabbed. How does that sound?"

That information seemed to comfort him and he visibly relaxed. "Better. Thanks. And hey, at least I'm not an evil administrator."

"Thank goodness for that," Lyra answered. She went around the corner to get Arthur. “Seeing as this guy doesn’t have tentacles, you can sew him up, right?” she asked, handing him the new patient’s chart.

Despite Arthur’s worry about Lyra’s career being held back, it was he who was struggling with the last part of his residency because of his irrational fear of cephalopod surgery.

He nodded and disappeared.

Lyra went back into the waiting room and turned to say something to Gorb. She was interrupted when a guy wearing a Halloween costume bumped into her. He spilled a red liquid on her white doctor coat. “Oh no,” she said, “Are you okay?”.

“Sorry about your coat,” he said. He was wearing a cape but not a mask. “It’s not real blood. You bumped into my spare fake blood vial.” He held up an empty plastic vial. Then he held up a partially bandaged hand. “Well, this is real blood, but I didn’t get it on your coat.”

Lyra rubbed her face with her hands. “We’ll get you fixed up,” she said. “Just so you know, it’s September. You’re a little early for Halloween.” She headed back to her apartment to get another coat.

Just another day on Celestica.

~

Gorb sat at his post at the front desk of the hospital waiting room. He glanced around the room which was, at the moment, mostly devoid of patients.

It was a happy room, though. And that was mostly thanks to

him for wearing down Grayson, the hospital Chief of Medicine, until he agreed to repaint.

In Gorb's opinion, all of the steel and cream and beige in the space station was emotionally debilitating. It had taken him only one boring afternoon to do the necessary research regarding the adverse effect of the boring former room color on his physical and emotional health. Then, once he got the psychiatrist to sign off on it, he was in business.

Within a week he had the okay to choose a color. He went with a very cheery, green, Limonade-shade that he loved madly. Partially because it was fun and different, but mostly because everybody else in the hospital hated it.

He flipped through the Deeper Spaces Accessory Guide magazine looking for some new jewelry. *No, no. Stars, no. What were they thinking? Already have it. Last year's product, no thank you.*

"Um, hello?"

Gorb knew who it was without looking up. There was, after all, only one other person in the waiting area. And having been here for several hours, he was probably irritated by now. It was Gorb's job to let him know that the delay wasn't his fault. Luckily, this was the part of the job that he really liked. He looked up at the guy and pretended to listen.

"Look," the patient began.

Gorb dug through a desk drawer and found a pair of horn-rimmed glasses. He placed them on his face, which was not easy, as he was a jellyfish and didn't have a nose. The glasses were not prescription. They were his looking-down-on-people glasses, and they came in very handy. This is where people came to wait. This was a hospital, not a Starbucks. *Oh, that's good*, he thought, I'm going to start using that. *It's simply the way things are*.

"I appreciate your feedback, sir," Gorb interrupted him. "But, this is a hospital waiting room, not a Starbucks. When you come here, you should be prepared to wait. You have a cell phone there in your hand to keep you occupied, or you could bring a book or a crossword puzzle. Anything to help you pass the time without getting all ragey on us hourly workers, ok?"

"Well, I still think I should have been seen by now."

"We are very, very busy and we'll get to you when we get to you. You got it, Mr. Gimpy Arm?" The glasses were sliding down so he pushed them back up.

Gimpy arm made a dramatic show of looking around the dozens of empty chairs in the room. "There's nobody else here. How busy can you really be?"

"Are you dying?" Gorb asked.

"What?"

"Are. You. Dying? Right now. Like, at this very moment?"

The patient just stood there and blinked. Gorb decided that now was the time to press the moment.

"Because if you're dying. And I mean dying right now, then I can press this little button here. Do you see it? This little red one that I almost never get to push. Because when I push it, then red lights start going off everywhere, and sirens blare, and very busy doctors come running from their very important current duties to save your life." He waved his jellyfish tendrils around dramatically.

Gorb realized he had the guy going. He smiled, a very subtle gesture that he could get away with because the humans never noticed.

"And if I press this red button, then you'd better be dying, because the doctors just love taking out those cool electrical paddles, you know, the ones with the noise that make the scary beeeeeeeeep sound? They're the ones that they use to bring you back to life. You've seen them on television, I'm sure. And you know what else? If you're not really dying and they do that stuff to you, it can actually kill you. And it also probably hurts a lot." He whispered that last part.

"But you know what?" Gorb put the glasses back on the desk as they simply wouldn't stay put in the middle of a conversation this fun. *Pity*. "My day has been extremely boring so far, and I could go ahead and push the red button if you want me to. You'll get immediate service."

He let his tendril drag dangerously close to the button. Then he looked up to judge the guy's reaction which was sheer, delicious panic.

"No, no. I'm not dying, okay? But like I put on the form, I'm in pain. I think my shoulder's dislocated or something. It happened when I was, um, helping somebody. Move something. Over to a new, um apartment."

Gorb tried to raise an eyebrow, but he didn't have one. "Sex injury," he said.

"Wh- what?" Gimpy arm stammered.

"Look," Gorb said, pointing. "I wrote it right here in parentheses, on your intake form. I put-*suspected sex injury*. See there?"

"Hey, that's not what I said. And it's not what I wrote, you idiot jellyfish."

Gorb grinned at him, floating side to side jubilantly. "I was right." He held out a tendril for the guy to fist bump, but he didn't.

"It's okay, man. I only sting when I want to sting. And somebody got lucky tonight, am I right? Well, in any case, you got lucky before you got hurt."

He held up a tendril again. The patient looked deflated and he exhaled. He gave in and returned the fist bump with his good hand.

"Right on," Gorb said.

"Can you please just erase that last part from the form?"

"No way. Altering patient intake forms is a class four felony. Very, very serious."

"But you altered it already!" He protested. "I'm just asking you to un-alter it."

"See this blue button over here?" Gorb asked. "This one calls security. You do *not* want me to push this one. Those guys won't come in here to save your life. Oh no. Listen, the fun is over. What you want to do is go over there, keep playing games on your phone, and wait until I call you. Or I swear, I will start pushing buttons over here."

2

Scythe stepped out of his ship, down the hallway, and into the space station Celestica. He looked around through the eyeholes in his mask at the metallic grey hallways. He smiled behind the mask, even though nobody would be able to see. He had waited a long time or this. Then he heard a voice.

"Welcome to Celestica. Can I see your ID?"

He looked around to locate the voice. It was coming from a thin, old looking orc off to his left.

"You need ID to enter Celestica," the orc continued. "Especially if you are wearing all black robes and a mask. I mean, you could be anybody, couldn't you? And it's not even Halloween yet." He shook his head before continuing. "Oh yeah, and I also have to ask, for this form here. Are you on Celestica for business or pleasure?"

"My name is Scythe," he said, "and I am here to free you."

"Okay," the orc said, smiling. "That's a new one. Free me from what? And what do you mean? Free me personally? Or is that sort of your weird crusade mission in life?"

He frowned suddenly. "You're not a telemarketer, are you?

Because let me tell you, even if you make it past me, that kind of thing is violently frowned upon here."

Scythe shook his head, causing his robes to flap. "What I am is more powerful than you could possibly imagine. And my offer to free you still stands. But this is your last chance."

"Great. Ok then. Neat, um, mask." The Orc said, but now the outstretched hand waiting for the ID was trembling. "I'm still going to need to see your ID card, though. You know, space station regulations and all." The Orc's finger stretched toward a button that would probably call security.

"I told you. I am Scythe. Lord of Kingdoms and Ruler of myriads." Unfortunately, the years of experiments he had spent perfecting his mind had left his physical appearance shocking to the normal beings in this universe, making the mask and costume necessary. Only until he freed them, however.

The orc's finger halted without pushing the button. He brightened. "Well, that sounds more like it. Some sort of celebrity, eh? Why didn't you just say so? Good for you. Just for the sake of asking, do you have to go to school for that kind of thing or is it like internet fame, where you sort of have to get lucky? Can I have your autograph? Your title sounds like something that would impress the young people."

Scythe sighed. This was getting tiresome and he had wasted enough time already. He reached a hand out in the direction of the Orc, but didn't make physical contact. He didn't have to. "Time's up."

The Orc gurgled an objection and dropped to his knees. Scythe finished him off. The Orc fell over and stilled. He wasn't here to reap old Orcs, he was hunting bigger prey.

Scythe made his way down the hallways of Celestica, ignoring the mildly shocked expressions as he passed.

"What, is it Halloween, already?" a passerby asked.

Scythe continued. These inferior beings couldn't help it. Before long he would show them the error of their ways. And when he freed them into his realm, the first thing they would learn is that their eyes deceive them. *My reality and my perception are so much better than their own.* They will thank him then, yes, they will weep tears of grateful joy.

Still, a brilliant plan is a brilliant plan. And his plans always worked. In fact, the beacon was already here and set up. Almost everything was prepared. And so, he made his way further and further into the gigantic space station.

He walked freely down shining metallic walls and past hordes of residents who did not yet know their master. Until the crowds thinned out and he continued alone, back into the furthest, remotest corners. And there he summoned to him what would hopefully be the last of the lesser-intelligent minions he would ever need.

He stopped as he approached them, and they mobbed him, squealing everlasting allegiance. "Yes, my pets," he said. "I have been preparing you from afar and now I am here. For now, I just need one of you. I will summon the rest of you when I'm ready."

He held out a hand to the volunteer and communicated his orders very specifically. The instructions were understood, and the hairy beast scampered off.

Now on to the next part of the plan, which involved finding a place to plug into a communications and intelligence hub.

He strolled off back toward the main part of the station, humming along with the soft music playing in the hallway.

3

Grayson walked the familiar grey hallways with a skip in his step. He had been to a million space stations. Well not really a million, but enough of them to know that the majority didn't have eight foot high ceilings and reinforced steel structure.

A lot of things could and would happen to a place out in deep space. The extra tall ceilings and comforting metal structure of Celestica were the main reasons he had taken the job here. That and getting kicked out of his old hospital.

He tapped his hand on the shiny metal hallway as he made his way to the Frenzy, the station's biggest and rowdiest bar. Normally he would hang out at the smaller bar right next to the hospital, but today was a slow day at the ER and he wanted to drum up some business. He considered that his job as Chief of Medicine.

Celestica was home to thousands of beings, many of them accustomed to a fairly tough existence. This after all, was Celestica, the famous space station at the edge of the galaxy's scariest black hole. Only the people who wanted to live dangerously made their home here. And of those people, only the bravest would ever set foot into the Frenzy.

He arrived at the giant wooden doors that had motorcycles carved into them. In front of the doors was a goofy werewolf wearing a white shirt, leather jacket, and jeans.

"How's it hanging, Carl?"

Carl grinned a jagged, toothy smile. "Always happy to see you, Grayson. You here to stir up trouble?"

"You know me."

"Go on in, it's been too quiet anyway."

Carl opened the door for Grayson and the wall of loud music hit him. He entered with a smile and a wave. "Thanks, Carl."

The Frenzy was a giant, raucous, place with antique weapons on the walls and solid wood décor, most of which had the nicks and cuts from a thousand bar fights. It was part Wild West mining saloon and part *Mos Eisley Star Wars cantina*. And despite the fact that he was longer in the tooth and paunchier in the center than most of their usual clientele, it was one of his favorite places. It was also the perfect place for occasionally drumming up extra hospital business.

He whistled even though nobody would ever hear it over the roar of rock music and approached the bar. On a space station there wasn't really a day or night, only shifts. That meant that there were always people at the bar, even in the middle of the day.

He glanced around. Right now, the customers were mostly roughneck orc miners, having finished up the night shift and ready to hit the hard liquor.

Grayson had barely had his morning donut, but he wasn't averse to a little bit of morning drinking, especially if it was for a good cause.

There were wooden tables scattered all over the large, rectangular room. The walls were decorated with old swords, guns, and all manner of clubs that were visible in the dark club with blue spotlights.

He had heard rumors that some of them, the ones nearest the top of the ceiling, were worth a pretty penny, having been used by assorted unseemly individuals. Those were the objects he usually stared at when he came in.

At the center of the room was a three-hundred-sixty-degree, circle style bar that always had at least three bartenders on duty. He made his way to it, sat down on a wooden barstool, and ordered a Slick Fifty, having to shout over the noise.

"A little early in the day for that kind of drink, don't you think, Grayson? You're never up to any good when you order those." The pretty bartender winked at him.

They had a little thing going, but probably only in his head. "You know me, I like to live on the edge."

"I do know you," she said, sliding his drink over, "try to stay out of trouble this time."

He held his hands up in mock surrender, then grabbed the glass off the bar and took a sip. *Delicious*, as usual. He swirled the liquid around the cup and looked around. A sudden push from behind made him lurch forward toward the bar and grasp his drink tighter.

"Hey," he said, turning around.

A seven-foot-tall lizard glared down at him. "Watch it," the lizard said.

Grayson recognized him, he was a troublemaker named Larry. "You bumped into me," Grayson answered, unwilling to back down from the beast. The minute you roll over for these guys you're in real trouble. He did have to crane his neck to look up at him, though.

As far as the trouble part was concerned, this was going to be even easier than he thought.

Luckily, he still wore his lab coat everywhere with his Chief of

Medicine nametag, not that anybody could read it in here since it was so dark.

He found his white jacket to be useful in these types of situations because if things did come to blows, people were less likely to hit a doctor, or they'd at least pull a few punches. He thought about escalating the situation, but it was too soon and would be easily traced back to him, something he was looking to avoid.

Also, he was getting a reputation. Subtlety had never been one of his strong suits, but he was going to have to think of another way to stir up trouble today. A simple bar fight wouldn't do.

He took another sip of his drink and carried on. The beast decided to let it go. Looking around, he found that today was actually pretty quiet for a change, just like Carl had said.

He was actually seriously wondering how in the helios he was going to be able to cause a disturbance without sticking out like a sore thumb, medical jacket or not, when an actual disturbance broke out in the back of the room.

It started with a single shout, enough to draw everyone's attention. Grayson turned toward the sound and heard more shouts. A chair hit a wall and splitered. There were more screams. *Now we're talking.*

Grayson squinted to see what was going on. The disturbance looked like it was centered around an orc miner gathering in the back, which wasn't at all surprising. This time looked different, though. And now, others from around the room were joining in. Maybe this was his lucky day after all. *It can't be my fault if I don't even know what's going on.*

Turning back to the bar, Grayson saw the wide eyes of the cute bartender in front of him. That was odd, because usually they were unflappable. The bartender ducked underneath. That meant that she was either going to hide, which he doubted, or to grab a weapon, which was far more likely.

He took a sip while he waited to see what would happen next.

Ah, weapon. He was right. He couldn't help but wonder why she had bothered to grab the weapon. What made this bar fight different than the hundreds of others he had witnessed?

He turned back again toward the fray and followed the wide-eyed and now armed bartender's line of sight. That's when he saw what looked like a dog at first, but it wasn't moving like a dog. He squinted to get a better look and could have sworn it was a rat. The only problem was that it was too big to be a rat.

Small animals like rats, bats, and other pets were an inevitability on spaces stations. No matter how well you checked each visitor, people were always sneaking them in. Then the pets escape or sneak off and breed. Then whammo. You got rats.

The rat in question waddled to a central open area in the middle of the room. Illegal weapons were being pulled out all over the place. Now it was Grayson's turn to be concerned.

No, you idiots, he thought. You can't all draw on a rat that's in the middle of a circular room. Even if half of you hit it, then everybody else will still be vulnerable to live fire in a room full of bystanders. Armed, idiot bystanders, but fairly innocent nonetheless.

He had wanted to come in here and drum up a bar fight, but with fists. Broken bones, maybe a couple of lacerations or bumps on the head. Nothing serious.

"No!" he screamed. "Don't shoot, people." Since the only thing he could do about the armed idiots at this point was wait and see if they really were dumb enough to shoot each other, his mind went to another question. How had this space rat grown to the size of a dog? Was that even possible?

He frowned and took another sip of his drink, keeping an eye on the tense situation. Might as well.

The rat hissed at the growing crowd and flashed its teeth. *Here we go*, thought Grayson.

An explosion of weapons fire filled the room. Grayson dove

behind the bar along with the bartenders, shielding himself from any stray weapons' fire.

The bartenders sat calmly waiting it out. They weren't new to any of this. In fact, they all appeared to have assigned spots. One of them was even carving today's date into the wood, adding it to a very extensive list.

Grayson watched the bartender carve with a small, curved blade. The knife was so exquisite that it nearly distracted him from the raging laser battle going on a few feet away. Then, as quickly as it started, it all died down. Well, the weapons fire ceased. That's when the screaming began.

"Hey Grayson," the bartender said, as they all emerged from their hiding hole. "I think they're going to need you."

Grayson peeked out from behind the very solid wood and stared. The rat was indeed dead in a pool of blood in the center of the room, right where he had been.

Grayson went out for a quick look around. Several orcs and a couple of other species were wounded, although they looked like they were going to be okay.

"Okay everybody," he said, moving closer to the rat and raising his voice, although it was unnecessary. The music had stopped the doctor's coat now had all of their attention. "I'm Grayson, Chief of Medicine at the hospital that many of you will be visiting shortly. I have a few questions first, though. How many of you shot yourselves in the heat of the moment?"

Only one person raised their hand.

Idiot, that was a trick question.

"How many of you were shot by other people who were aiming for the rat?"

More hands went up.

Grayson cursed and took out his phone. He called the ER to prep extra doctors and nurses. When he hung up they were all still looking at him. "Okay, boys and girls, what have we learned about firing our weapons at an object in the center of a circular room?"

There were mutterings.

"Oh yeah."

"That makes sense."

"Now he tells us."

"Think people," Grayson said, shaking his head.

Well, he did, in fact, drum up some hospital business. Or at least he had found it anyway. And there was no possible way this could ever be traced back to him or considered his fault, so he was clear with both the space station and the hospital's lawyers, so he supposed all was well that ended with still living residents and dollar signs.

The only thing bothering him now was the giant, suicidal rat. What was the deal with that? He dialed his phone again.

"Hey, Floyd? We have a situation at the Frenzy. No, I had nothing to do with it. Oh yeah, the cause of the disturbance was a giant rat. The dead thing is still here in the middle of the bar. Just jot down in your notes that we are going to run some tests on it, okay?" He listened for a moment and then answered. "Yeah, sure, if you want. You certainly could put it that way, a giant mutant rat started a bar fight at the Frenzy." He hung up.

When he looked up from his phone, he realized that nearly everything in the Frenzy had gone back to normal. The music was back on, the lights seemed even dimmer, and the uninjured had gone right back to what they were doing. Except, of course, for the injured people and the dead rat. Unbelievable.

"I'm sorry people," he announced, "but I'm afraid for the next few minutes your normal routine is about to be interrupted. I need the music off and the house lights on."

There was a general groan from the crowd.

4

Lyra accompanied the procession of doctors and nurses as they moved in a hurried way down the hallway toward the Frenzy bar. Luckily, she had time to get a new coat before the emergency. Normally the halls were pretty crowded this time of the morning, but the residents were smart enough to get out of the way of the craziness coming at them.

As the Frenzy came into view, both double doors were open awaiting their arrival and all of the lights were on inside. Lyra had been there a few times and was not aware that the place even had real lights.

Now she knew why the lights were always so dim.

The place was gross. The tables weren't clean, and it looked like it had been a week since the place had been vacuumed. *Ew, I've eaten in here*, she thought.

Grayson stood just inside the double doors as they entered. "Get a move on, people! That little trip took three times longer than it should have."

"Thanks for the pep talk," Lyra answered him. There were still clumps of people gathered at tables at the far end of the room. They looked like the hard-core patrons who were willing to wait out the medical emergency in order to get back to their drinks.

Wow, Lyra thought. It was pretty typical for Celestica, though. The residents here had seen it all and usually took going with the flow in the face of an emergency to a new level. It actually made things easier most of the time.

"Just for that, you and Arthur get to take care of the dead rat," Grayson said. His wrinkled, bony finger pointed in Lyra's direction.

"What dead rat?" Lyra asked, looking around nervously, hoping he was joking.

"Hey!" Arthur said, "Why me?"

"Because you're standing next to her."

"Seriously, Grayson? I'm your best doctor and you're going to have me collecting an already dead rat?"

"Yo. I'm right here," Vax said. "The best doctor is already saving people while you guys are yacking."

"Stuff it Vax," Lyra said.

"Have you looked at it?" Grayson asked Lyra, ignoring Vax and everything else that was going on. The place had gotten very busy.

Damn. His new question about looking at the rat threw her off. She'd had a very good sarcastic remark ready, but now it was gone. Grayson had that effect on people.

"Have I looked at what? The rat?" *Damn.* She'd had a very good comeback ready, but now it was gone. Grayson had that effect on people.

Grayson scowled at her. "No, have you seen all of the disgusting stains in the back of the restaurant. Of course, I meant the stupid rat."

That can't be good, she thought. She glanced at Arthur and then around the room, locating the area with the rat. Then she headed toward the disgusting rat carcass at the obvious center of the disaster area that was, unfortunately, very clearly lit.

She made her way through all of the splinters and debris to the smelly, oily, gray body that was adding its own permanent disgusting mark on the establishment as its blood soaked into the carpet.

The thing was huge. It had to be at least forty pounds. If she wasn't looking right at it, she wouldn't have believed it. And then there was the smell. It was like hair and death and body odor combined to form a type of chemical weapon. She covered her nose with her lab coat.

She knelt down to examine it further. It had at least ten different bullet holes and was missing half of its face. Between the gross carpet and the hairy beast, she took a moment to keep her breakfast from coming up. "Okay," she sing-songed, trying not to breathe. "I looked at it, are you done torturing me now?"

"Not by a long shot," he snapped back while also directing traffic as patients were loaded onto gurneys and preparing to head back down the hallway toward the hospital. "What is different about that thing, Lyra?"

"It smells bad?"

"Don't get smart with me."

"It's an unusual size?"

"Exactly. I don't like it. I've never heard of one so big. It's got to be at least, what, forty pounds?"

"Maybe it's just a rat-adjacent species? Maybe an overfed pet? Who in the name of exploding stars cares?"

"I do," he answered, "let's get it back for testing."

"You gotta be kidding me. What are we supposed to put it on? A gurney or an appetizer tray?"

"As it so happens, I had this brought over for you to put it on." He handed her a stiff looking parchment paper looking rectangle with handles on both ends.

Her gaze shot back to him. "You're going to make me touch it and then carry it all the way back? Are you crazy?"

"Not you," he answered, "yous. Plural. Both of you. You and Arthur. That's what you have gloves for, dearie."

Ugh. She glared jealously at all of the other doctors and nurses who were treating actual patients. *Ugh.*

That's when Arthur jumped into action. He accepted the offered improvised carrying device and set it down next to the rat. Then he wrestled the thing onto the mat. Unfortunately, the only way to do that was to turn the thing from right-side up with the blown off head to upside down with all of its insides exposed and paws pointed in the air in all different directions. Its mouth was open and its tongue was hanging out. *Again. Ew.* Still, she was grateful to him. "Thank you, Arthur," she said.

"What's the matter, Lyra?" Grayson taunted. "You're a doctor. You see this stuff all of the time."

"Yeah," she said, "but it usually doesn't smell this bad. And I don't do particularly well with rodents. Seeing as we never have rodent patients. Hey!" she said, realizing something. "Arthur, how are you doing this?"

"What?" He looked up as if he were very happy to have been temporarily left out of the conversation and was visibly uncomfortable at being sucked back in. "What did I do?"

"You can't even operate on cephalopods, and here you are, just fine with a disgusting rat?" She had to admit, he was braver than she gave him credit for, and she would have to give him some of the brownie points he so greatly desired for taking point on rat duty.

"I'm not weirded out by rats," he replied simply. Then he grabbed his end of the makeshift rat gurney and nodded to her. "Ready?" he asked. "The sooner we get this thing back to the hospital, the sooner you can be done with it. Maybe. Unless you're going to make her do the necropsy?" He looked up at Grayson.

"You wouldn't dare," she said to Grayson.

"Don't worry," he answered, "I'll have plenty of other things to keep you busy once you get back to the hospital," Grayson said.

Lyra nodded to Arthur and lifted her end and they made their way past the still-gawking eyewitnesses and out the door. All she could think about as they lugged that idiot thing back to the hospital was how Arthur could deal with giant rats and not normal, everyday cephalopods.

In fact, there were several Cephalopod nurses and doctors and they all had volunteered to help him get past his fear, but for now he was still resisting. It was the one discipline keeping him from completing his residency. He had been stuck for months. She looked at him as they went, which she could do because he was busy concentrating.

"How about hypnotism. Have you considered that?"

He raised an eyebrow at her. "It's a good idea, but I think this patient is a little too far gone for it to work."

"Smartass," she said. "I mean for you. Uh, for your Cephalopod aversion. And I thought you were dying to get off of this space station and back to your girl or something."

"I don't know," he said.

She expected him to say more, but it was a touchy subject for him. "Look," she said, "I'm only saying it because in my opinion you are a fine doctor, despite what I said this morning." She grinned. "I want you to be able to move forward with your life."

Lyra was out of brownie points, so thank goodness that's when they burst through the bay doors of the Emergency Room waiting area.

~

Vax and Nancy were busy working on a Frenzy patient when Grayson materialized in the doorway, making Nancy start.

"I wish you would stop doing that, Grayson."

"How are you two kids doing?" he asked. "Stitching up the nice bar patrons, are we? Any problems?"

"None," Vax said.

"Yeah, that about sums it up," Nancy answered. Just when she felt like she was getting a handle on the situation somebody else appeared in the doorway. She did an angry double take. *I'm trying to work here.* But it was just Lyra.

Lyra stood in the doorway with her arms crossed boring holes into Grayson with her eyes. "Your giant, hairy, disease infected menace is sitting in research waiting for whatever weird party you have planned for it, Grayson."

Then Lyra continued, "Anyway, funny how Grayson here just happened to be at Frenzy, again, in the middle of a chaotic event that involved injuries," she said.

"Hilarious," Grayson added. "Except it wasn't my fault this time. Ask any of the eyewitnesses."

"Likely story," Lyra continued. "While all the other doctors got shiny new patients, I had to lug the giant hairy rat down to research."

Lyra was barely paying attention to them anymore, she was looking down at her phone. "Okay, I gotta go. So, in conclusion, enjoy your rat, Grayson."

5

Astrid paced around her new room that functioned as both her home and office. It was the second biggest room on the space station. If she was going to live here, she needed lots of space, and now she'd got it.

It had taken a full six months, but she had finally gotten the room just the way she wanted it. Now she could concentrate. It wasn't that she hadn't been doing her job in the meantime, she had. After all, she was a professional.

What life boiled down to in the end, though, was enjoying your own space. If you could make it your own, then you could accomplish anything. It's the creed she hocked in her self-help books, and she believed it fully.

She looked around approvingly. The room now sported new earth tone carpeting and hand-woven accent rugs. Exotic art hung on the walls, and there was a ceiling surround aquarium with neon fish. The aquarium was her favorite idea and a stroke of genius for this particular space.

Unsure how she would react to living in a completely manmade environment, the added attention to detail of the glowing, living creatures calmed her right to sleep at night.

Yes, this will work. Her living space was perfect, and in the back was her office where she could see clients. She let herself enjoy the moment, also one of her principles for living.

As she moved between the living and working areas of her apartment, she caught sight of herself in the carefully-placed confidence mirror. The bottom half of her, of course, was beautiful shiny blue tentacles, while the top half was gorgeous dark-haired, fair-skinned, green-eyed goth girl. *Oh yeah*, she thought, *still got it*.

That done, she crossed the room and sat down behind her desk and looked at her to-do-list, going in the usual order: highest paying clients first. She dialed the video chat number. A dark-haired man with a serious five-o-clock shadow and a red fedora appeared on the screen.

"Vincent, hello. You are a strong, brilliant, confident man. How's it going? I said you'd be the first to know when I had settled in, and now it's happened. So how do you want to do this? Online?"

Vincent, on his end of the video chat, looked around nervously and shook his head. "Astrid! How's my all-time-favorite goth Cecaelian? Online doesn't work for me," he said, "you know that. There are too many people listening in. How about we meet here on Galderbash?"

"Can't do it," she said cheerfully. "Not allowed in that system."

"Wow, bad girl, eh? How about we meet halfway then, on Orion Eight?"

"Nope."

He raised an eyebrow. "Is there any place within a few dozen planets that you are allowed to meet me?"

She took a long, cleansing breath and then let it out. "Let's not focus on that," she replied. "Look, you're a guy that doesn't like online interaction because he, um, values his privacy, right?"

He nodded.

She had no idea what it was that Vincent did for a living, but she knew it wasn't legal. That wasn't something they had discussed as of yet, and she wasn't about to ask him. She made it a point never to judge.

Furthermore, she wasn't going to tell him why she was now banned from most of the civilized galaxy. Her law enforcement issues were not relevant to the matter at hand, which was her paid services. And what she was paid for, was in fact, to break down ideas and motivation to the bare necessities and then repackage them in a new and effective way, sort of. And she was good at it. A lot of times that involved a significant amount of thinking on her feet. She got an idea.

"I know that you do not ordinarily like stepping out of your comfort zone, Vincent. I also realize that I now happen to be farther away from your normal garden variety portal service. But you are a man that has the means to travel by private channels, and when I tell you where I am, I have a feeling that you will agree that it is a perfectly acceptable place to meet."

Vincent looked dubious. "Ok, try me."

"You may not believe this, but I'm on Celestica Space Station." Then she smiled and sank back into her expensive faux leather chair. She waited for the information to sink in.

"You don't mean *THE* Celstica. Outside of the civilized galaxy?"

"Yup."

"Near the edge of the supermassive black hole?"

"That's the one."

She could see the wheels in his head turning now.

"That'll work for sure. Your terms are acceptable. What we'll do is the garden variety sessions online and the, um, more specific monthly sessions at your new office. And I'm on my way, right now, for the initial session."

"I figured you'd say that. You know me, I'm full of great ideas."

"Of course," he said with a wink, "that's why I pay you the big bucks."

Astrid hung up and sighed happily. *Yes, this place is going to work out just fine.*

That done, she switched on the television to her new favorite comedy, *All The Things That Motherboard Never Told You.*

Floyd crossed two of his four arms over his green chest and squinted at the tablet.

He was very aware of the guest in his office squirming in the chair opposite him. The squirming was good. Squirming meant he was distracted and in a hurry. Floyd glanced up at him. He was a hulking guy, not quite werewolf build, but very hairy. In truth, Floyd had no idea what species Lorn Dakks was, and he didn't care. All he cared about was getting the timing right.

"It only took me fifteen minutes to read my portion," Mr. Dakks said. "You've been on that thing for twenty-five minutes." He looked at his watch to double check the elapsed time and settled into an angry glare.

"Look, Mr. Dakks," Floyd said. "I gave you your time, now you have to give me mine. You do want this done correctly, no?" Glancing up at the digital clock in the left-hand corner of his office, Floyd did his own calculations. Two more minutes, then he was in the window.

He flicked through the pages of the lawsuit on the tablet. He tried his best to look serious, concerned even. Got to make this look right, or they catch on to you quick. *Almost time*. He ticked off the seconds in his head. *Four, three, two, one. And now.* He scribbled his name onto the bottom of the line on the tablet and slid it over to Mr. Dakks.

"Mr. Dakks, I am reasonably sure after looking everything over that everything should be to your satisfaction."

Mr. Dakks looked down at the tablet and then back up at him

again. He looked wary for a moment, like he could sense something was up.

Floyd played it cool, rapping an index finger on the fake wood desk and letting the noise reverberate around his office. This was his space, his domain, his turf. And he would be darned if he was going to let some guy just walk in and legitimately sign a lawsuit against his hospital.

It was important to keep up appearances though. He held up his hands in mock surrender. "Hey, you don't have to sign it if you don't want to." He didn't risk another glance at the clock. He only had another ninety seconds or so before he'd lose the advantage.

He sat further back and smiled. The smile wasn't at Mr. Dakks, though, it was just a general smile. He lived for this. This was his high stakes poker. Most gamblers would risk tens, hundreds, or even thousands of galactic credits on a card game. This game was worth thirty-four million credits.

He drummed his fingers on the desk again in an attempt to look bored. In this case, looking at his watch might actually help, so he did. Then he got an even better idea. "You think it would be easier for you if I look away?"

"You guys are going to pay for what you did to me," Mr. Dakks said and signed it.

Floyd listened for the submission noise, which was music to his ears. He looked at his watch. He had thirty-five seconds to spare. *Victory.*

This guy was suing them, nothing he could do about that. What he could do is make sure that the paperwork was signed just outside of the civilized boundary of the galaxy. And it just so happened that his office rotated out of the boundary for several minutes at a time once every four-point-five hours.

By the time Mr. Dakks got back to his home planet and had his lawyers look over the contract that was legally pristine in every other way, it would be too late and the damage would be done. The location, date, and time stamp snafu would add ten

years and thousands of galactic credits to h
obstacle could be rectified of course, but t
went way down. Never bet against the house.

The poor guy stood up, certain he had
that, I'll teach you to be more careful wh
species that are outside the top four thousand most common without knowing exactly what you're doing."

"Once again, sir, I apologize for that. However, you were brought in after you apparently lost a fight with the back end of an out of control star destroyer. The EMTs found you severely injured on a cement landing platform. Your fellow employees testified that you were under the influence of something. And also intoxicated by something else. And also naked. Frankly, you were in such bad shape that nobody could tell what species you were when you got here. You were minutes away from death, and that is the reason that the surgeons didn't take more time deciding which exact organs were most precious to you in which exact order in the carnage. You should thank Vax for putting the functioning organs back in as well as he did."

"Oh yeah, that reminds me. You'll find an emotional suffering clause in there." He pointed at Floyd for emphasis. "A Krull Warrior surgeon? You know what I think? I think you put him there just to frighten me out of suing. Well, it didn't work, did it?"

"No, it did not." When it came to patients like this, Floyd wished that he could let Vax be Vax sometimes, but that was another situation entirely. "But I assure you, as Chief of Surgery, Vax is second to none. You were lucky he was there when you came in."

"I don't feel very lucky these days," he said, tapping in the information to email himself the completed contract. "I can't wait to get off of this piece of junk and back to normal civilization." He got up and stomped off.

They can have you, Floyd thought.

And that was why it was made very clear in writing upon

ng Celestica that all lawsuits had to be originated in this ice and with Floyd's knowledge, if not consent. It also stated that once any lawsuit contract was signed by both parties, the papers could be emailed, faxed, or shoved up any orifice the ex-patient wanted, because by then it was way too late.

6

Arthur paced around the doctor's lounge. It was the only place on this god-forsaken space station at the minimal safe distance from a supermassive black hole that he actually liked.

And that was mostly because of the gorgeous floor to ceiling windows out into space. The view was breathtakingly beautiful, except that the thousand blinking lights were a constant reminder that he wasn't where he was supposed to be. And that he wanted to get back.

The rest of the lounge simply looked like an expensively decorated college dorm. There was a smattering of good quality, but mismatched chairs, tables, and sofas that were scattered around and a couple of televisions mounted on different walls.

To his left, a human girl named Emily and a squid-like creature played a board game he didn't understand. They pushed brightly colored crystals around a spherical board with their minds. Arthur wanted to give it a try, but he was embarrassed to ask how it worked. He was unsure if it was A.I. enabled or if it required actual telepathy, which he obviously lacked.

A giant, hulking warrior doctor sat in front of the television with his feet up, guffawing loudly at what looked like creatures falling into a hole set to silly music. His name was Vax. Of all the Krull species in the universe, Vax was the only Krull doctor that Arthur knew about. Arthur had the sneaking suspicion that Vax was only here to make the rest of them feel inferior.

A tingle of fear ran through Arthur's body every time he was in the same room with Vax. Every time. Three months on the space station had not made things any easier in that regard. It didn't help that Vax usually carried a sword around.

Arthur had asked about the sword once, going as far as suggesting that it was a very bad idea to let an already terrifying doctor carry a lethal weapon around with him.

The disappointing answer he received pointed out that the sword was both Vax's emotional support object and it also had religious significance, and as such it was not subject to normal, common sense restrictions.

That's when Arthur heard a chirp. He turned and saw the robot. The robot's name was MACRO. MACRO was silver and roundish and had red eyes. The robot's eyes were capable of glowing a piercing Rudolph the Reindeer red, or so he had been told. He also had a cool looking blue fin on his head that made him look vaguely fish-like.

MACRO made a different chirpy beep this time. It was a lower pitch.

Vax stood up. "You people heard MACRO, there's an ambulance coming."

"Hey, Vax. Why does MACRO's chirp sound different," Lyra asked. Lyra crossed to the little robot and knelt down to look at him.

Vax just shrugged and turned off the television.

Lyra was a human in her late twenties with a sandy brown ponytail. To Arthur she was equal parts terrifying, attractive, and comforting. The comforting part came from her ability to usually know what to do when things went wrong.

Arthur ran to the window and searched for an approaching ambulance ship. "I don't see anything."

Emily stood up from her game with a nod to her opponent. "No offense, Arthur, but you've been here three months, and MACRO's been here for years. And of the two of you, MACRO has never been wrong. You're right though, Lyra, the chirping sound is a little off today. A higher pitch, maybe?"

"No offense taken, but it doesn't seem like any of you even technically know what he's saying," Arthur objected. "He could mean anything by that chirp."

"He means there's an ambulance coming," Emily continued. "Look, when MACRO was made, I think I remember somebody bringing the robot manual up here. Maybe that's how we learned the basics of his communication. If you're so interested in it, maybe you should just find the manual."

Find the manual, thought Arthur. Find the manual and understand the mysterious robot. That was the best idea he had heard in the three months he had spent here trying desperately to kill time.

That was when the room alarm sounded, indicating that new patients were inbound. Emily's words bounced around in his head. MACRO was always right. And Arthur was going to figure out MACRO.

"Alright," Vax announced. "New guy, you're with me." Vax indicated with his head that he was talking to Arthur. "The rest of you are on standby."

~

Arthur stood in the Emergency Room waiting area. The familiar red flashing lights accompanied the alarms, which bothered Arthur. *How are we supposed to concentrate with all of this racket?* Almost on cue, the noise and lights stopped as two gurneys burst through the door and into the room.

In this case, there were two patients being hovered into the room by the EMTs. The EMTs were hornet-like creatures. They were buzzing specifics at Vax and the nurses and pretending like Arthur wasn't even there. Unfortunately, that was something that Arthur was starting to get used to.

Vax and a nurse named Nancy took the first patient back toward the operating rooms. As they passed, Arthur could see that the patient looked to be in bad shape and looked barely conscious.

There was another patient though, and Arthur was next in line. He stepped forward to draw the hornet EMTs' attention. They seemed even more animated than usual. Their antennae gestured wildly in the air while they buzzed loudly.

Arthur watched for a moment, trying to put his finger on exactly what was different. The buzzing was gibberish to Arthur, who cursed himself for forgetting and pushed the auto translator button on his watch.

Everything changed as soon as the translator kicked in. That's when Arthur understood the extra concern. The second patient was one of the hornet EMTs, and her name was Mandae.

Arthur leaped forward upon figuring this out and grabbed the gurney. His hesitancy was always because he was afraid that a patient he was expected to treat would be a Cephalopod and he had a severe phobia that was hampering his career.

But this hornet EMT was right in his wheelhouse. Arthur had done an Insecta specialty in med school. The patient wasn't conscious and had what looked to be a crushing injury, but it was something that Arthur would be able to take care of as long as there were no extenuating conditions.

"Hello. Mandae? It's Arthur, I'm going to take good care of you, okay?"

Arthur looked to the hornets who were concerned about their coworker. They were staring at him.

"I'm sorry," Arthur said, pointing at his watch. "I just got my translator turned on, could you tell me again what happened to her?"

"She took a baseball bat or something to her thorax in the melee," one of the hornets buzzed loudly.

"What melee?" Arthur asked.

"We got a distress call from Serebus moon. When we got there, we found the patient and started rendering aid. He was in bad shape, barely alive. We were in the middle of getting him ready for transport when we were attacked."

"You were attacked while rendering emergency aid?" Arthur couldn't believe it; that was terrible. "Who would do that?"

They continued buzzing at him. "We think the attacker was there to finish off the first patient." The antenna pointed in the direction Vax and Nancy had gone.

Arthur stopped and stared. "Who attacked you?" *There were rules after all,* Arthur thought, *even in space. Even this far out into space and nearby a black hole. You don't attack medical professionals rendering aid. You just don't.*

"Just treat Mandae," they screamed, still overly agitated.

Arthur stared down at the thorax wound. "I can fix her, ok?" Arthur said, hoping to calm them down, but they turned back to stare at the door they had barged into just a few moments before. Like they were waiting for something.

Now Arthur was extra confused, so he wheeled Mandae off toward a room. Chances were, he wouldn't understand all of this until it was over anyway. That was the way that these things usually went.

Mostly he just did what he was supposed to do until the excitement was over and then waited for somebody to explain it to him. The least he could do was help Mandae. He hovered her down the hall and toward the operating rooms, picking up a nurse along the way.

Just before he disappeared around the corner, though, he heard shouts and saw a tall, furry creature burst into the waiting room. The hornets went crazy, buzzing at what appeared to be a werewolf who was wielding some kind of bat.

Arthur pushed Mandae faster. If that maniac was after her too, then he wasn't going to take any chances.

The last thing he saw was Gorb scrambling for a weapon and shouting into his com. "Security! We need security to Emergency Room Intake. Code 44. Code 44. You heard that right, Code 44. Crash, this means you!"

7

Nancy set up shop with Vax in Operating Room number three. It had the standard layout as the other operating rooms, but slightly enhanced technology data. That was due to a recent lawsuit that Vax had been on the receiving end of. As much as Vax annoyed her, though, that one wasn't on him.

She started switching on some of the new technology and considered her place in the universe. She was always stuck with Vax, seeing as she was the only nurse who had been able to overcome her fear and loathing enough to be able to stay in the same room with him for more than five minutes. She shook her head, sometimes it just didn't pay to be professional. Especially if that meant getting stuck with the one guy that everybody's afraid of.

Vax shook his head. "Wow, this guy is in bad shape, who does that to an EMT? And a baseball bat? How urban caveman is that?"

That surprised Nancy. "Hey, you're talking? You walk around with a sword scaring all of the patients, most of the doctors and nurses, and even ancillary civilians. How is that any different?"

"I've never bludgeoned somebody into being one of the

patients?"

"Touché."

Nancy caught Vax just in time. "Don't cut him yet, Vax, or Floyd's going to kill us."

Vax paused. "Cutting helps me think. Hurry up, you worthless fool."

Nancy tapped furiously into the computer-sized scanner to get it ready. "See, that type of thing is exactly why nobody else will work with you, despite your position as Chief of Surgery."

He frowned. "What's wrong with the way that I speak?"

"Only your tone, words, and attitude," Nancy responded. "Hey Vax, how many appendages? Heads? Eyes? Tentacles? Help me out here."

"Looks garden variety human to me. I don't care what this guy looks like under his clothes. Besides, it's way more accurate to just scan him than for me to guess."

"That's what you said last time and it got us into trouble. And that's not what you say when you're all, 'I'll just cut into him and see what's what.'"

"Hey," Vax said, "he's moaning, maybe he can talk. Hey buddy, what species are you? Any artificial bits in there that I should know about? You better start talking or I'm going to cut you wide open and take a look inside. Ok?"

The patient passed out.

"To fix you," Vax added. "I'm only going to cut inside to fix you." He looked at Nancy. "Why do they always do that?"

"Maybe you should have started with that bit about saving him. And to answer your question, because you're a scary guy, Vax. Nobody believes you're even a surgeon, you're from a warrior race that's got thirteen systems worried to within an inch of their lives. In fact, why are you here again?"

"To save lives. By cutting people. I'm a cutter not a fighter, you know that."

"Why can't you understand that doesn't make any of us feel

very much better? And yes, you keep saying that, but why? Why medicine? Why do you have to be brilliant and awful at the same time?"

"Why can't you just scan the patient so that I may cut into him without getting into trouble?"

"Okay, it's up and running. Out of the way!" She grabbed the portable analyzer from its dock on the side of the species scanner and ran to the patient, pointing it at his abdomen and pulling the trigger. There was a weak, mechanical beep, and then she ran back to the scanner to get the readout.

"Ok, we're dealing with a humanoid-adjacent species with twenty-three percent of its body mass replaced with artificial parts. He does appear to have some internal injuries, so you get your wish this time. Congratulations, you get to cut him open."

Vax whistled. "Twenty-three percent is pretty high. I don't think I ever asked if you had any AP, Nancy?"

"You wish. I know you didn't just ask me about my body Artificial Percentage."

"What?" he asked. "I was simply making conversation. It's not that big of a deal, for instance, mine is just under five percent."

Nancy crossed the room to the patient and Vax started the procedure.

"This ought to be a piece of cake for you, Vax. I hope that poor EMT Mandae is going to be ok."

Gorb bobbed excitedly. He was at his usual spot at the hospital waiting area check-in. The doctors had disappeared with the patients and the hornets had beat the werewolf guy back toward the ambulance bay.

He rummaged through the bottom left drawer for weapons.

"Hey," said a patient, "what's going on here, am I in danger?"

"You heard what happened," Gorb said, "you were sitting right there pretending not to listen to everything when it went down. You can stay or you can go. But don't pretend you don't know what's going on."

Gorb paused to look up at the patient and grinned. "And in case you think you can stay here, fake an injury, and file a lawsuit, then you don't know Floyd very well."

The patient got up and ran out the door, toward the main space station.

Gorb laughed, causing the room to shimmy for him. Well, it was he who shimmied, but it made the whole room a cooler place.

Gorb paused his search for a weapon, knowing that if there were anything interesting in those drawers he'd have found it years ago. He waited for a few moments before deciding that it had gotten entirely too quiet.

He floated over to the door and put his head to the side in order to listen. He held his breath.

Without any warning, the door slammed open. Luckily, Gorb was able to float out of the way on the breeze that the door made when it opened.

The room went from deadly quiet to screaming loud in an instant. How was that even possible?

Gorb watched as a werewolf burst into the room with no shirt and dirty, ripped jeans. He would have liked to focus on the werewolf's hideous lack of fashion sense, except the creature was wielding a baseball bat and was making headway despite having a dozen angry red sting marks on his body and hornets currently buzzing around him.

Gorb recovered himself, and zoomed over to the werewolf, extending his tendrils to an exposed part of the intruder's leg. Sparks flew. After all, he didn't need a weapon, he was a weapon.

The werewolf's face distorted in pain, but he still kept going. Gorb couldn't believe it seeing the physical punishment he'd already taken. "*What is this werewolf on, anyway?*"

Arthur wasn't in the room with the EMT patient for very long when Lyra burst into the room and closed the door. "What have we got?"

Again, Arthur was used to this sort of intrusion. "An EMT who was attacked. Blunt force trauma to the thorax."

"What?" Lyra asked. "You're kidding, right?"

"I think the attacker just burst into the waiting room when I wheeled her in. You didn't see anything unusual in the waiting room? Like a big, crazy, werewolf guy with some sort of weapon in his hand?"

"I came in the back way," Lyra said. "Did you call security?"

"Gorb did, he was calling out the code 44."

Lyra pressed her head against the door. "I don't hear anything. What do you think is going on?"

"No idea," Arthur said. "And it's a good thing because I'm a little busy here. Maybe the hornets beat him back. Or maybe Crash showed up."

"Maybe," she said. She watched him work. "So, you're a no-go with the squids, but you're fine with rats and insects, then, eh?"

Arthur shook his head. "How long are you going to mess with me about that?"

"Shhh," Lyra said.

"You can't shush me," Arthur replied testily, "you started the whole thing."

Lyra gave him a savage look. "Shush. I think I hear something."

"Huh?" He paused with the scalpel and looked up. "What are you talking about? What did you hear?" He whispered it due to the shushes and the severity of the look on her face.

He didn't have to wait very long to hear what it was she was talking about. The screaming and scraping sounds were getting closer and closer.

"What the-" Lyra whispered. She cracked the door open and peeked out.

"No," Arthur said, "don't do that, you'll draw attention to us."

Lyra shut the door quickly and attempted to lock it, but the operating room door did not have a lock on it. There was typically not a need to lock people out of surgery and only a couple of secure rooms had doors that locked.

"He's coming!" she whispered.

"Who's coming? What are you talking about?" he asked, scalpel still held above the patient.

"The werewolf, of course. I think it's him!" She cracked the door open again. Something he wished she would stop doing. "It looks like he's still got the baseball bat. Where in the helios is Crash? You said they called security, right? Oh no."

"What is it now?" Arthur asked and then regretted it. He wasn't sure how the situation could get much worse.

"Gorb's hanging on to him, along with the hornets. They're trying to slow him down. And they're not having much success. He's heading this way. Little guy's going to get himself killed. Luckily, he's okay right now because the werewolf appears to be distracted, but we'd better do something quick."

"We?" Arthur swallowed.

"You're right, sorry," she said, running around the room rifling through drawers. "You can't help, you're in the middle of surgery patching up the EMT. Hey, do you know if we have anything that could be used as a weapon in here?"

"I don't think so. Why in stars would we keep weapons in an operating room?"

"Well, there's got to be something here that will help," Lyra said. "Look, they're doing their best to slow him down, but they're losing ground fast. And what if he's still after her?" She indicated Madae. "What if he's come to finish the job?"

Arthur wasn't used to this level of stress in the operating room. He started deep breathing.

Lyra looked like she was trying to make a decision. "You said that the werewolf attacked both patients?"

Arthur thought about it. "They said that they believed that he was after the first patient, Vax's patient, and that Mandae just got in his way."

"That doesn't bode well for Gorb," Lyra said.

She stood holding her breath with her back against the door like she was going to hold it shut against an onslaught. She held up a hand. Things had gotten quieter, like the storm of noise outside had passed.

She turned her ear toward the door again to listen. Then she risked another peek outside. A nearby pounding noise startled both Arthur and Lyra. She closed the door again.

"What's going on out there?" Arthur asked.

Lyra's eyes were wide. "The werewolf went right past us. I guess he wasn't after the EMT after all, he was after the first patient. He's pounding on the door where Vax and Nancy are. He's trying to get in."

"What do we do?" Arthur asked.

"You save Mandae," she said.

"What are you going to do?" Arthur asked. "Don't go out there, Lyra! Or at least call security first and make sure they're somewhere close."

"On what planet is calling Crash again going to do any good?" she shot back. "He should already be here. And we're out of time."

"At least Crash has weapons. I mean we're under attack here. I think." He shook his head. "I don't know what's going on."

"You operate." She went back to one of the drawers and grabbed a scalpel. "I'll see what I can do."

"That werewolf is dangerous, Lyra. He's already injured two people."

"I'm aware," she said, and quietly slipped out the door and closed it.

8

Things were worse in the hallway than Lyra thought. The werewolf was still going, despite looking like a character from a horror movie. From the looks of it, the hornets had done a lot of damage. Ditto for the jellyfish who had put untold volts into the werewolf in just the few seconds since Lyra had exited the operating room. She could see sparks emitting from around the werewolf's jeans.

You've got to be kidding me, she thought. *There's no way that hairy guy should still be moving*. She had to duck as she heard another hornet EMT come buzzing down the hallway to help.

Despite the stinging, holding, and insect bites, the wolf just kept coming. He dragged everybody down the hallway with him, baseball bat in his hand, toward Vax and Nancy's patient.

Lyra looked down at the scalpel in her hand, suddenly having doubts as to whether adding stabbing to other current events was going to help anything. Was there anything she could do that wasn't already being done? Then it hit her. I have to warn Vax and Nancy.

But if she went in there, wouldn't this guy know where to go? He'd just follow her. But he already knew where to go, because he passed the first operating room. She frowned. How did he know to go past the first operating room? Then it hit her.

"He's tracking the victim, somehow. Has to be."

Lyra made a decision.

She screamed, sprinted past everybody and into Vax and Nancy's operating room. She slammed the door shut and threw herself against it.

"What in the name of drug addled stars is going on out there?" Vax demanded.

Lyra sucked in some breaths. "The, um, suspect. That did that to him," she pointed at the patient. "Well, he's outside the door right now. And he's trying to get in. And he still looks murderous. And kind of supervillain-y. I had to warn you. Gorb and the hornets are doing their best to stop him, but nothing they do seems to be slowing him down."

"That's a very unlikely scenario," Vax said. His voice didn't sound certain, but he was obviously having trouble believing the situation was as dire as she was making it out to be.

The door rattled with a vicious bang, and the doorknob tried to turn. "Tell that to him!" Lyra screamed and tried to keep the knob from opening.

Vax put down the scalpel and rummaged around behind him. He produced a full-sized sword.

Thank goodness, thought Lyra. Vax's thinking sword. He always had it with him.

"Nobody breaks into my operating room," he said with a gleam in his eye. "Stand aside," he said to Lyra.

"But, you don't understand how strong this guy is," she objected, and then wondered why she hadn't just stepped aside for the nice guy with the sword. *That would have been a better idea, Lyra.*

The argument became moot when the door flew open and off of one hinge, but not the other. Thank goodness, otherwise the patient could have been seriously hurt. Lyra was thrown from the doorway and onto the ground. She scooted backward on the floor away from the menace. She knew if anybody had a shot at stopping him it was Vax anyway.

The monster paused in the doorway, scanning the room, presumably for the exact location of the patient. Then he took a step forward and raised the bat high in the air, continuing to ignore the jellyfish and the hornets.

Crash appeared in the doorway behind the werewolf. Crash was a giant, hulking, scaly predator-looking creature. There was a loud bang and a light flash as his blaster fired. The weapon blew a hole right through the middle of the hairy creature, who dropped to his knees and then fell face forward onto the ground.

With a last-ditch effort, the werewolf rolled over onto his side and shook his hairy head. "You don't understand. You should have let me kill it," he said, and then he finally stopped.

“I told you people,” Crash said, “I’m all the security this space station ever needs,” and then he walked away.

“It took you long enough,” Lyra shouted.

9

Ian grinned his most charming grin into the computer at the thousands of people tuning in to his latest live web show.

"Hello, world. It's me, Ian, welcoming you to Fear Zone Universe. That's right, F.Z.U., the show that takes you live to the scariest, most dangerous places in existence. I go to them, so you don't have to."

He took a quick sip of water while he ran the video intro before continuing. "Fear. The most primal of motivations. Have you guessed my location yet? I have a very special set of shows coming to you from the one and only Celestica. That's right, people, the space station at the edge of the deep, dark, terrifying black hole. As usual, I come to you from the most terrifying places in the universe to prove a point. And the point is that I'm still here."

He indicated dramatically to the window behind him. "Behold the view. You can't technically see the black hole, but it's there. Although the thrill for all of you at home is nothing compared to being here in person. If you get the opportunity to visit Celestica in real life, I highly recommend it. Personally, I'm starting to enjoy it here and am thinking of extending my stay. My research into aggregate intelligence systems is going even better than I had hoped. For some reason, the algorithms are very different here and so far, the results are fascinating. That's all the teasers you will receive from me right now. New episodes are coming soon, so stay tuned, people. These are going to be some of the most exciting shows ever recorded in F.Z.U. history."

The grin faltered and then disappeared completely before one last parting shot. "One more thing. Feel free to come join me at any time."

He hung up. *I know they won't.* He was pleased with himself. Of all the destinations he had been to in the last few years, this was by far the most adventurous. The most dangerous. And the most sexy.

His mind raced right back to Lyra. He texted her a copy of the webcast. She was the one person here capable of making his life even more fantastic. *Send.* Now all he had to do was find something to do while he waited for a response.

~

Vax sat in the doctor's lounge. In his favorite comfy chair, the one that happened to be in front of the giant window. With his feet up. He got a text notification.

It was the official, hospital will die immediately if you don't respond to this text in three seconds or less notification, which he had set on his phone as a cheery little chirp.

He had all of his text prioritized by sound, something he was able to accomplish only after being at the hospital for a while and sorting out the panic-natured individuals, even among his bosses, and those prone to overly dramatic overreaction.

Unable to punch the hyperbolic text senders, he could at least prioritize them in the order of which he considered their importance. And his importance was not necessarily their importance, which meant that they all thought that their emergencies were of the utmost importance. That was simply the way hospitals were. That didn't mean he had to agree.

He waited a second to finish what he was doing. At the moment, that was staring through the giant window of the doctor's lounge, which he had to himself, toward where he knew the black hole was. This was a pilgrimage he made often when he believed the place to be empty.

Vax's Krull race had a deep-seated fear of black holes. Black holes and little else. Well, maybe doctors. The thought made him chuckle. That's why he was here. In order to get away from them, all of them, he had to face his deepest, darkest fear.

No, not face his fear exactly. Facing the fear implied that he'd fly past a black hole on a daredevil mission. This was more like living with his worst fear. And it had done something marvelous to him. In the early days, he had done massive amounts of research about supermassive black holes. How they behaved, stability probabilities, dangers and timelines.

What he had discovered at the end of it all, waking up every morning just the same, was that he was okay. They were all okay. Everybody simply thought they were crazy, but they weren't. This part of space should be stable, even for the next few millions of eons. Stable and secure. What most of the tourists and Krull considered inordinately risky hotdog living, he now considered home.

He raised his coffee to himself and took a slurp. Yes, if he was going to give up warmongering and conquering to be a rebel doctor, as he had always dreamed, then he would do it in style. And if any other of his race ever set foot here, it would be they who were afraid.

The text notification sounded again, same as before. He sighed contentedly and drank in the view for one last moment. Then he actually read the text. Three seconds later, he was out the door.

"What's going on here?" Vax asked, sprinting into the room. "I got the notification, but it didn't say what was wrong."

"I'm not exactly sure," Nancy said, looking at a computer readout screen.

Vax grabbed the charts and checked the readout of the steadily beeping machine. They were both silent for several moments. Finally, Vax spoke again, "He should be recovering."

"He is recovering. Physically. It's his brain waves, Vax. Something's going on with his brain waves. They're not acting normally."

This caused a new search for files from Vax who muttered something along the lines of, "Why didn't you just say so in the first place" and "I will destroy you when all of this is over."

"What did you say?" Nancy asked.

"What? Oh, nothing. Just looking for the patient's brain wave information. My text notification looked like it came from the Chief of Medicine, but I'm assuming now it was from you."

"I know that you rank your texts by importance." Nancy replied.

"I rank my texts by the order of the importance that I place on them, not the official order of importance. And for the record, I'd have answered yours sooner. You make more sense to me than that old, bloviated, should-be-put-out-to-pasture-"

"Howdy, folks. What's up?" Grayson, the Chief of Medicine, appeared at the door.

Nancy whirled to see Grayson standing there. *How in stars name was he able to keep sneaking up on them like that?* She wanted to tell Vax that it wasn't her that called him, but Vax glanced at her face before he even turned around toward Grayson and she knew that he knew. Sometimes he was easier to work with than the human doctors. And sometimes he was a terrifying pain in the ass.

"Grayson," Vax said. "What are you doing here? I'm busy."

And sometimes he's not easier to work with than human doctors, she thought.

"Hello, Grayson," Nancy said. "You're late to the party. All of the excitement and danger was a few hours ago when we were nearly attacked. This has nothing to do with your rat bar fight, this is the one with the weird patient being pursued by the murderous werewolf. We're okay, by the way, but Crash could have gotten here way sooner. It would be great if you could speak to him about hiring more people. Now that you're here, is there something that you need?"

"Just being nosy," he answered, poking around the stack of charts, "that's my job, being Chief of Medicine and all. Besides, something is going on in here, I can feel it. I'm a quarter telepath on my dad's aunt's cousin's side, you know."

Nancy knew for a fact that wasn't true. Vax looked up at him wide-eyed, wondering.

"What's up with this patient's brainwaves?" Grayson asked at last, looking up from the wrong set of charts.

Nancy giggled. "You were outside in the hallway eavesdropping, weren't you? Vax, he's not really telepathic."

Vax exhaled.

"If I knew that sort of thing would have bothered you, Vax. I'd have done it sooner," Grayson deadpanned.

"Here!" Nancy said, finally finding the correct readout. "What do you make of this, Vax?" She handed him the sheet, and Grayson gave her a dirty look. "I also have it right here on the screen, Grayson, you can take a look too."

He crossed and they all stared at the data in silence for a few moments. Then Nancy went to the patient himself to observe.

Most of the measures of progress were there including steady heartbeat and improvement of wounds. Sure, she would have liked to have seen him regain consciousness by now, but all in all this seemed like nothing out of the ordinary. Except for the brain-wave patterns, of course.

Then there was the lack of identification. Normally, especially this far out in the galaxy, everybody had identification on them, even the scofflaws. It was required. Even the werewolf with the baseball bat had his I.D. on him. They found it easily after Crash shot a hole in the middle of him.

She observed the patient again as she counted his breaths over the course of thirty seconds. Just fine. Hmmm. *How am I supposed to contact your family if I don't know who you are?*

The patient opened his eyes wide and sat up fast enough to make Nancy jump back.

It took Nancy a moment to recover from the shock of it all. Not to mention the heebegeebies she got. She took a deep breath and leaned forward.

"Sir? You're in a hospital on Celestica Space Station. You didn't have any ID on you. Can you tell me your name or give me a number for somebody to contact?"

The patient didn't answer. He just stared blankly for a moment without blinking and then laid back down and closed his eyes. In fact, he laid back down so quickly and matter of factly that Nancy started questioning after a moment whether he had even sat up at all. "You guys saw that, right?"

"I saw it," Grayson said, "and now I need clean underwear. That was creepy as hell."

"Ew," Nancy said. "What do you think, Vax?"

Vax turned his attention from the paper back to Nancy. "I think this brain activity data is inaccurate."

Nancy shook her head. "I don't think so."

"Then how do you explain it?"

"I can't. That's why I showed it to you. Grayson? Any ideas?"

Grayson frowned his best I'm-thinking frown and pretended to look at the screen again. "Unless this guy is a chemical zombie or an illegally artificially intelligent zombie, or a robot designed to mess with us, then no. This data certainly doesn't make any sense. One minute his brainwave activity is off the charts, the next minute it's flatlining."

"Be serious, Grayson," Nancy said, "this isn't one of your daytime television shows." At the moment, Nancy wished she was in a daytime soap.

"Look, you're brilliant," she said to Vax, "and you've been around the block a few dozen times," she indicated Grayson.

"Offense taken," Grayson responded.

"If you two can't figure out what's going on, then who can? Because according to that data right now, his brain wave data is off the charts. Not only should he be conscious, he should be bouncing off the walls. I've only seen that type of activity once before, and that was when a hyper species came in here hopped up on Blue Pixie."

Vax frowned. "I guess we'll just keep an eye on him while we try to figure it out."

There were moments like these that Nancy was glad she worked with Vax. He may act violent and cocky and better than everybody, but that's how they all acted, and besides, at least he was logical and easy to predict. That thought sent her spiraling about life choices.

Her mother had told her, "Stay on planet, find yourself a nice guy. Don't go running off to haunted space stations." But did she listen? Oh no, and now she's here working with a Krull surgeon near a black hole.

10

Emily entered the examination room with the giant rat. *Why does Grayson hate me? This isn't just hate, either. This is the definition of a hostile workplace environment.*

She adjusted the mask over her mouth and nose. She had doubled it up just in case. And also wore two pairs of gloves.

Thankfully, this wasn't a full necropsy. The hospital just wanted a few tests run on the thing because of its abnormal size, possible communicable disease, and its intelligence as it related to the possibility of starting a bar fight. "Did you hear that, rat? You started a bar fight, now you get to be famous."

"And now I'm talking to rats. Thanks a lot, Grayson. I guess I'll start with the brain," she thought, and took a deep breath. She needed the saw and cursed Grayson some more. Then she thought she heard something out in the hallway as she rummaged around looking through the drawers.

"I hear you, Gorb." She couldn't be a hundred percent sure, but she figured she could just make out the swishing sound that he made when he was lurking around the hallways. She waited for a moment and listened to make reasonably sure he was gone. Satisfied, she turned back to her task and found the saw.

She glanced down at the rat and pulled her gloves on tighter. *Ew.* Its stomach was engorged, although that could have been due to the half a dozen bullet holes. The head was smaller in proportion. It had weighed in at an incredible forty-eight pounds.

She paused for a moment. Then she went to the computer in the corner and looked up everything she could find on different rat species, even the effects of deep space on rat species.

All the while she was keeping a wary eye on it, as if it would at any moment jump up and bite her. She shook her head. *Stop it, Emily.*

If she could find a logical explanation for this giant horror, it would help her to sleep better tonight. And also, to keep her lunch down.

A few minutes later she gave up, having no such luck. There were no records anywhere of giant, nearly fifty-pound rats running around on space stations. Maybe it was a cross-breed or an outlier. She could hope. For now, she decided to go with that. She grabbed the saw again and took a breath.

She cut into its head to the tiny pea-brain to take a look. *What the-?* The brain was huge. And also discolored. Instead of a pale pink color, the brain was a bright, neon blue. So blue it was glowing. She frowned.

On a hunch she went over to the wall, keeping an eye on the rat, and turned off the light. The rat brain did, in fact, glow in the dark.

You gotta be kidding me. What could it mean? Maybe it means I do a paper on this and get famous. Do I really want to be famous because of a neon rat brain paper, though?

She focused and took a closer look. The rat's brain was highly abnormal. Well, technically, this was the first rat brain she had ever seen in person, but according to all of her research, this rat brain was massively above average size, and also a very abnormal color.

"Hmmmm," she muttered out loud. "I wonder if this

abnormal color could mean a trace amount of residual brain activity?" She realized she was talking to herself, but this was a strange situation that warranted it. This rat's brain was glowing in the dark, for heaven's sake. She got the brain scanner and hit the button. Then she looked at the data. Then she hyperventilated. According to his brain, this rat was still alive.

She looked down at the beast with his head blown off and more than a dozen bullet holes. The black tongue was hanging out of its mouth. "What is going on here?"

Freaked out now, she took the samples that Grayson ordered quickly. Except for the brain itself, the rest of the tests came back completely and wonderfully disease free. Thank goodness. The one thing she needed to do now was to contact Grayson. And then intergalactic disease control. Even though the other tests came back normal, the abnormality was big enough to trigger next level attention. And that was before the crazy brain scan.

~

Lyra arrived early at the restaurant to scope out the place, but soon realized that Ian had beat her to it.

"Hello again," he said with a grin. "So glad you could make it to dinner." He was wearing a perfectly fitted black suit with a tasteful but splashy orange tie. The outfit certainly worked for him. He was tall, tan, and had closely cropped, curly dark hair and had the confidence of an intergalactic video blog star. Which he was.

He led her though the elegantly decorated restaurant to a table in the back with a perfect view of the stars. He held the chair out for her and then sprinted to his own.

"So, did you see the video I sent you? It broke records in several different systems. I gotta tell you, I love this space station. The danger, the mystery, the very hot doctors."

Oh, he's good, Lyra thought. She stared at him for a moment.

Complimenting the station was the smartest thing a newbie could do around here. At least, to her. And then there was the hot doctor thing.

"I saw it," she answered, "and it was good. Lately, I'm more interested in your little science project, though."

The waiter appeared, and in the end, after some fun back and forth, they both decided on signature steaks and a more than satisfactory bottle of wine. Lyra had never been to this restaurant before, and looking around the place, she was impressed. There were nearly wraparound windows with peaceful views of stars.

Inside the windows, cozy tables with beautifully decorated tablecloths dotted the landscape with plenty of room in between to allow an impressive amount of conversation privacy. A quick glance around revealed that he had cleverly reserved the best of these tables with the most beautiful view of both the stars and the beautiful, glowing, nearby moon.

A stunning, blue Cecaelia walked by, accompanied by a guy in a red fedora. She couldn't help but stare. In a space station full of strange creatures, that was the first time Lyra had ever seen a Cecaelia. *Half octopus, half goth-human, she thought. That's pretty cool.* The guy in the fedora was just a guy in a fedora.

She turned her attention back to Ian. The bread came while she was looking around and he was tucking his napkin onto his lap. She did the same and grabbed one of the rolls. They were still warm.

"So, you have your science project and your web fame, I've been meaning to ask you, which came first?" she asked in between bites.

"Well, that's a funny story, actually. I'd have to say it all started with me trying to get thrown out of grad school."

Lyra raised an eyebrow. "Alright, that's a point to you. That's how you start a story."

He smiled. "As I said, I was in grad school, and I wasn't entirely sure that I liked the direction that my life was going. So, I tried to think about the most outlandish, crazy thesis I could come up with for two reasons. One, so I could basically waste my own time thinking about what I actually did want to do with my life and two, so that when I presented the thesis for my masters, I would be laughed out of the room."

That's when the steaks came. Lyra waited for the food to be set down and the waiter to leave. "Okay, go on."

Ian was already digging into his food. "Oh yeah. Where was I?"

"Trying to get laughed out of the room presenting your thesis. And I have to say, there was probably an easier way to get out of grad school."

"I don't know," he said, "nothing came to mind at the time. Anyway, even though the thesis was crazy, it was fun enough that I actually spent more time researching it than I thought I would."

"Okay," said Lyra, pausing from her food to take a sip of wine. "Are you going to tell me what this crazy thesis was? And what all of this has to do with your video blog fame?"

"I'm getting there," Ian said. "Because they're connected. You see, I decided to research the effect of location on algorithms. Specifically, the effect of the spookiest, most haunted places in the universe."

"No way," Lyra said. "You're just messing with me now."

"Honest," he said, raising a hand like he was taking an oath. They both giggled. "There's no way I could make this up. And I'm fully aware of how crazy it sounds. That was the point, remember?"

"Okay. Fair enough."

"So I go in to present my thesis. I had slides and everything. I only had enough money to research the one haunted place nearest my home planet, but sure enough, there were actual fluctuations in the data. I still expected to get laughed out of the room, but on some level, I felt that I had not completely wasted my time."

"So, they laughed you out of the room and you proved them wrong by going out and becoming a famous web star?" Lyra asked.

"Way worse," Ian said. "They gave me the degree and threw a bunch of money in grants at me to go and do more research."

Lyra paused, wine glass in her hand. "You're kidding."

"Nope, all of this is one hundred percent true."

"Wow, so, you failed at getting kicked out of grad school?"

"Yup. And then I started traveling the universe getting weird data in spooky places."

"That sounds kind of fun actually. What about the web stuff?"

"Well, that started on a dare from my roommate, who was too chicken to visit the haunted moon of Vermilion. He said he wouldn't believe that I was actually there unless I live-cast it. So I did. And then I put it online. And then it just took off after that. It made me orders of magnitude more money than being a scientist, so when the grants ran out, I just continued to visit and live-cast from creepy, haunted places for money."

That's when the waiter came back with a dessert menu. Lyra got the chocolate mousse, while Ian went for the brownie sundae.

"That sounds great," Lyra said. "I have a question, though. Why still do the math if you're famous and have lots of money?"

"Turned out, I did like spooky algorithms after all. Now it's just a fun hobby."

Dessert arrived and they dug in. Ian caught her sneaking a glance at his brownie sundae and offered her a bite, which she accepted.

"That's not to say I don't like the spooky stuff. In fact, I think my favorite part of this webcast was the bit about the fearless nature of the people who live and work here. If there's been one aspect more fascinating than math about scary places, it's the people who live there. I meant it," he said. "You people fascinate me."

"You people?" Lyra raised an eyebrow.

"You know what I mean," Ian said. "The residents here. You're brave and you know it, don't pretend you're not."

"Why? Because we choose to live near a fairly stable black hole? You do realize that it's stable and the chances of anything bad happening in the next several hundred eons is very, very slim."

"I know. I looked it up. But as I said on the video, fear doesn't have to be rational."

"Tell me about it," she said. "For instance we have a resident, fabulous doctor, mind you, but he has a hang-up and it's keeping him from moving on."

"We all have hang-ups, though don't we?" he asked.

Lyra thought briefly back to earlier in the day and the stupid rat. Fear of gross, mutant rats was perfectly rational though, and up until today had not ever held her back in the workplace. "Absolutely. I have plenty, giant mutant rats for one, but back to my friend. He can't operate on Cephalopods. They freak him out."

"What was that about rats?" Ian asked.

"Nothing," Lyra answered.

"That's interesting about the cephalopods, though," he said, and she could see the wheels in his head turning. His video show was sort of an intelligent fear factor meets motivational speaker. Maybe fear of Cephalopods was something he hadn't covered.

"That's a new one for me," he said as if reading her mind. "There are a lot more beings in the universe attracted to tentacles than repulsed by them."

"You?" Lyra asked before she could help herself.

"Wouldn't you like to know," he said playfully.

That's when her phone buzzed with a notification from the hospital. She shot him an apologetic look and then glanced down at the phone.

"I'm sorry, it's the hospital. I have to check it."

"By all means," he said. "Duty calls, right?"

She read the message and then looked up. "I'm sorry, Ian. I have to go." She held up her phone for him to see. *Emergency Meeting in fifteen minutes: All Upper Level Hospital Personnel. Lyra, this means you.*

Ian shook his head. "Grayson, eh. He doesn't usually call meetings this late at night, does he?"

"No," Lyra admitted.

"Why the extra part on the end, just for you?" he asked. He looked inquisitive not accusatory.

"Oh, Grayson and I go way back. Before he was Chief of Medicine and way before I ever qualified as Upper Level Hospital Personnel," she answered. "And in addition to that, he's just a cranky old pain in the ass."

"So you two have a history?" he asked.

"You could say that," she said, standing up from her seat. "See you soon." She gave him a kiss and then made her way out of the restaurant.

11

Lyra was among the last of the summoned personnel to arrive. She wondered what could be so important to warrant an emergency meeting this late at night. The last emergency meeting was during the day and had to do with a machinist strike on the station.

"Now that everybody has arrived, I have an announcement." Grayson shot Lyra a look about being the last to arrive.

She rolled her eyes fast enough so that he'd know it had happened. *Damned if I do and damned if I don't*, she thought, knowing full well he wouldn't be giving her such a hard time if he knew she was out on a date.

"As all of you probably know by now, a large rat caused a disturbance at the Frenzy nightclub earlier today." He searched the eyes around him, presumably daring them to say something about his coincidental presence there, but everybody knew better than that by now.

She wondered what the deal could be with the rat. Was it carrying a specific communicable disease? Was she about to be quarantined? What was going on? For the first time in her career, she was happy to be upper management so that maybe for once she'd know what the helios was going on.

She also found herself hanging on Grayson's every word, which was doubly unusual. Most of all, though, she was happy that it was Arthur and not herself that had touched the thing. *Sorry, Arthur.*

His pause was too long for her to take. "I'm sorry, what about the rat?" she blurted out.

"I was getting to that," he said, "stop interrupting."

Everybody shot her a look so she stopped talking and took a step back.

"Anyway, the rat that was the center of the disturbance was found to have unspecific mutant properties. We are not quite to the point of a full quarantine on the space station, but we are looking into specific abnormalities."

Lyra's head was spinning. Mutant? Abnormalities? Other than being huge, what was the big deal here?

Vax mercifully broke the silence.

"For star's sake, Grayson. From what I hear it was simply a giant rat? Why the extra concern and the cloak and dagger act?"

"I can't tell you that right now."

Now Lyra was mad. *You call us all here to freak us out, especially those of us who were close to it and then you refuse to answer questions? Lame.* "Are those of us who happened to be in close contact with the weird, giant, mutant rat in any immediate danger?"

"Inconclusive," he said.

Now he was just pissing her off. "For heaven's sake," she said. "Why call us here and worry us if you won't answer any of our questions? What's the whole point of that?" She cringed for him to unload on her, but he didn't. She wasn't sure if that made her feel better or scared her on a whole different level.

"Good question. Glad you asked. This one I can actually answer. Because I had to. If you ask me, it's nothing. Just some good old fashioned intergalactic bureaucratic I-dotting and t-crossing if you ask me. How's that? Does everybody feel better? Breathe, people. There will be no personal time granted tomorrow. Now go home, get some sleep, and deal."

For the first time in her life, Lyra decided that one of his stupid meetings actually ended too quickly. She turned and headed back to her apartment, but she wasn't at all sure about the sleeping part.

~

Lyra was unable to get much sleep after Grayson's weird rat meeting the night before. She grabbed some coffee and made her way early to the doctor's lounge in the morning. This morning the room was packed.

Arthur was there sitting in the corner, but he tried to get her attention as soon as she walked in the door. She headed toward the back of the room as usual and collected him on her way.

"Hey, why are all the upper level doctors so agitated this morning?" he asked.

"Because we all had trouble sleeping," she responded truthfully.

"All of you?" he asked, his face scrunched up. "Together?"

"Not like that," she said. "Um, Grayson called a late mandatory meeting. Kept us all up. Being upper management isn't all fun and games," she said, rifling through the first of the very old filing cabinets.

That brought another frown of concern from Arthur. "Forgive me for noticing, but usually you just sulk with your morning coffee in the corner by yourself. Why are you searching through these old cabinets?"

She took a deep breath and a sip of coffee and wished him somewhere else. She blinked. It didn't work. "Since you're so observant, what exactly makes you think that I want company this morning? Because, spoiler alert, I don't."

"What are you looking for?" he asked, undaunted.

Why couldn't he ever be daunted, anyway? Then she remembered that he had also expressed an interest in the robot, MACRO.

The other morning, when it had emitted its weird, new beep it had made her wonder. And then they were attacked. Maybe it was related. Maybe MACRO was trying to warn them somehow. And now, in addition to needing something to do to keep her mind off the giant rat, she was more motivated to figure out what the heck the little guy was up to.

She glanced at the robot in the corner, who didn't give any sign that he acknowledged her presence. She doubted he could help at all with the medical mystery, but that didn't mean that there would be no advantage to understanding him. His arrival at the station and how he came to be in that robot body and why he hung out in the doctor's lounge was the stuff of mystery and legend. There were only rumors. From Grayson. That meant that none of the rumors were particularly responsible.

"Actually," she said, "maybe you can help me. You expressed interest in MACRO. You wanted to understand him, right?"

Arthur glanced at the robot himself, his spiky orange hair moving with him and then back. "Yes. Seems like a good idea. My other question is why he spends all day in the doctor's lounge. Is he, in fact, a medical doctor?"

"Doubt it," Lyra answered. "That's your question, eh? My question is why Grayson stuffed him into that ancient, obsolete robot body. Every other robot on board the station does things and communicates."

"No offense, MACRO," she mouthed the words at the robot in case it was listening. There was no response.

Lyra sipped her coffee before continuing. "I spent considerable time last night researching his model number." *Because I couldn't sleep because of the possible rat contamination and my close proximity to it. Damn it, Grayson, are you trying to get me killed?*

"And I couldn't find anything anywhere on the internet for that particular model or any related ones either." A piece of her wondered whether Grayson created this robot just to mess with her, but he was far too busy, lazy and self-absorbed for that.

"What I'm thinking here, is that whoever turned the robot on would have needed the manual for sure. Because the other rumor is that he didn't arrive in robot form."

"He's a *converted* robot?" Arthur asked, mouth agape.

"Close your mouth and try to keep up. I don't know the answers or if the rumors are true." *I just need something to distract me from the rat.*

"So, what'll it be, Arthur? You in or out? If you're in, pick another filing cabinet at the other end of the room and dig in." She pointed to the far end of the room. "If you're out, then still go to the other end of the room. I'm busy." She turned to fix him with steely eye contact. "And if you tell anyone about this, I swear."

"I won't, I promise."

And then, thankfully, he disappeared.

Lyra spent the rest of the morning until her shift sifting through very old documents in even older cabinets in between coffee refills and bathroom breaks.

Grayson had these old filing cabinets brought in here years ago when he had his office remodeled and never wanted them back. So here they stayed, stacked against the walls like old sentinels of useless knowledge from the beginning era of the hospital and in the case of some records, the space station itself.

Lyra may not have found MACRO's instruction manual yet, but she was finding other odds and ends that were, in fact, interesting.

For instance, it looked like the space station itself was infused with some very strange mathematical "spells", if you will, at its christening for some reason. She wondered if that had anything to do with what Ian had been talking about last night as far as his altered math algorithms.

Mathematical magic. Weird. The idea of it made her head hurt, but the concept seemed pretty interesting. She made a note to ask him about it and took pictures of those particular files with her phone before moving on.

A little while later, she changed tactics and decided that any document interesting enough to take a photo of would go in a manila folder she had gone to records to retrieve. Her morning at least felt productive, even though it was probably just odd, busy work.

She had taken at least a dozen documents that had caught her eye, including anything she found interesting about the birth of the Celestica space station. She gathered her new folder, having just enough time to drop it off at her apartment before going to work.

"You hang in there," she told MACRO across the room. "I'm going to figure you out."

MACRO, as usual, didn't respond.

"Ok, buddy. We'll talk later, I've got to go to work."

12

Floyd hit the refresh button on his email and wondered if his day was going to get better. His office seemed particularly dreary today. He looked out his window to confirm. *Yup. Gonna be one of those days.* Usually for him to be having this bad of a morning, the hospital was getting sued. That always made him angry. *Refresh.*

There was that little bit of excitement yesterday, when the hospital was attacked by a baseball bat wielding werewolf. That was a first. Crash had to shoot him. Right in the operating room hallway. Crazy stuff.

Floyd considered the danger of the situation. He could walk into a situation like that himself if he wasn't careful.

That revelation had sent him to the fun, seedier areas of the space station where he had procured for himself some powerful and illegal weapons. If he was ever in the line of fire for this space station, he may as well be prepared. *Refresh. Refresh. Nothing.*

He patted his locked, bottom left drawer newly stuffed with weapons. That's right, in the future he would be ready. Whether it was rampaging emergency room crashers or angry would-be litigants sitting right here in his office, he would be standing up for himself.

Nobody was walking all over Floyd anymore. Who knew you could stand up for yourself without having to trick people? No wonder people loved weapons. *Refresh*. Something new!

Floyd squinted at the email. He read it slowly. Then he read it again. He thought about this new problem and frowned. He wished that this new concern was as simple as being sued. Even worse than getting sued was the uncertainty of maybe getting sued. Uncertainty was the worst.

He re-read the email again and took a sip of coffee. Giant mutant rats. He shuddered. Well, one giant mutant rat, that had apparently started a bar fight.

Floyd figured if the rat was cool enough to enter a bar and start a fight, then it probably wasn't diseased after all. Although he was glad that he wasn't the one who had to get close enough to examine it. He did have to deal with the aftermath, though. He squirmed in his chair.

But yes, if push came to shove, then *rat started a bar fight* was a strong place to start with his argument that it was all in people's head. That was unless they got locked down on quarantine. He got a headache thinking about it. That opened them up to even more lawsuits, although smaller ones that had the capacity to take a long time and be painfully boring.

He tried to think about which one he happened to prefer. Gigantic, interesting, and newsworthy rat plague lawsuit or a bunch of ticky tack whiny I-was-stuck-for-a-few-days-on-the-space-station-that-is-my-home-anyway-and-was-mildly-inconvenienced lawsuit.

Fine, he thought. Spectacular rat plague was way more fun, left him more wiggle room to get out of it depending on natural causes. And the fact that they did employ exterminators on Celestica helped. And rat plague wasn't mind bogglingly tedious case law that had already been tried a thousand times and set in stone. It was shiny and new.

This made him smile, because although he had made up his own mind as to preference, he wasn't in charge. These things were always fluid, always a surprise.

Life here, if nothing else, usually found a way to throw stuff at him that he never would have suspected. And that's why he was still here after all of these years, practicing law at the end of the universe by a spectacular black hole. Because he loved a challenge.

A noise made him jump. Above him. There was a rumbling, running noise. It sounded like something was alive and running around the bones of the space station. He looked up in time to see a few specks of dust fall from the ceiling. So, he hadn't imagined it after all. This was new and worrying.

He grinned. It was time to call the exterminator. And also, to make a note of it, both in writing and in digital form, for later.

He dialed Maura. It rang. "Pest control, you got Maura." He explained to her what had happened and what he'd like her to do and what the ramifications were. He didn't leave anything to chance.

That done, he turned his mind back to his own rat problem and the email that he continued to stare at. It was very official looking and intimidating and had come from the Office of Intergalactic Disease Control and Coordination. IDC. Apparently, the doctor who had performed the necropsy had felt compelled to contact the intergalactic feds. Oddly enough, the email was not asking questions or gathering information, they were giving orders.

So who was this IDC person, BBasdhhhi, and what was this all really about? He knew that the only way to find out was to spend his morning doing research and making phone calls.

That was fine. That was how he spent most of his mornings. At least now he had something to do. There was one thing he wanted to do first, though. He wanted to touch base with the technician and find out what they knew about this whole rat thing. If he could get a handle on what he was in for, then all of this would go smoother.

He stood up, staring up at the ceiling at the spot where it sounded like something had run by. If there was even a possibility of more rats on the station, then he'd better find out in a hurry whether they were relatively safe or not.

~

"Pest control, you got Maura." She loved answering the phone this way. It made her sound like she was the head of a large department with tons of resources rather than a single person sitting in a banished office at the far end of the space station.

Truth be told, in space, there weren't an awful lot of bugs, so she didn't need a team. What she needed was very, very strong coffee so she could stay awake most days.

The voice on the other end of the phone call was Floyd, the space station lawyer. She had had a couple of conversations with him over the years on the phone, and only one conversation in person. Nothing of any particular importance, just odds, ends, and technicalities.

This time was different, though. She could feel the concern in his voice. An oversized rat. Possible disease infestation. We have to rule out contagion, that sort of thing.

It was worrying, but nothing she had not heard before. These types of pest problems popped up everywhere there were beings and food. The bar fight was new. How could a rat start a bar fight? And at a trendy bar like Frenzy? How'd he even get in? She had intended to ask Floyd about that, but he got another call and had to go.

Maura hung up. Now she had a purpose. Now it fell to her to do her thing. Investigate and report. That's why she got paid the barely minimum bucks. Hey, she wasn't complaining. She loved having an arsenal at her disposal and lots of free time to read and watch television. And every once in a while, when work did intervene, it was a nice change of pace.

She glanced down at the notes that she took from the phone call and decided she'd start at a garbage collection center on the far end of the station, just past the Frenzy nightclub. One thing was sure, today she would be getting her exercise.

She rummaged around her arsenal. Only a few light weapons were necessary for this first foray, which would be little more than a fact-finding trip. She stuffed the items in her pocket. A small ray gun, a species dropping test kit, and an extra-long extendable baton. The last item was the most used one in her arsenal which spoke to the usual level of danger that she was in, which wasn't very much.

That done, she grabbed her cup of coffee and headed out the door.

13

Maura made her way toward the trash collection zone for the Frenzy area of the space station. The collection zones were placed on the extreme edges of the station for obvious reasons.

So that one rat was big, she thought, *so what*? Rats had always been on the station. Still, the further down the deserted hallway she went, the more uneasy she felt. Up ahead of her, one of the hallway lights was blinking on and off ominously.

Figures. Easy, Maura. You're not in a horror movie. She reminded herself that just because she felt afraid, it didn't mean the fear was warranted, but she couldn't keep it from floating across her consciousness.

She swallowed hard and made it past the malfunctioning light. She hoped she would feel better once she got past it, but she didn't. Instead, she felt even further away from the rest of the station's inhabitants.

It's because you are further away, idiot, she told herself. People obviously don't hang out at the extreme edges of the station. That should probably make it safer overall, statistically speaking. She knew she was almost there now and picked up the pace. Soon, the large, iron trash receptacles were in sight. *Whew.*

She stopped, heart still racing, and looked around. The first thing she expected out here when she heard of a giant rat was that maybe these bins were overflowing, but they weren't. Everything appeared to be in order. And so far, no rats.

The next order of business was to check the trash bins themselves. She crossed over to them and took a deep breath. Then she lifted the heavy cover and peeked inside. *Nothing.*

She wasn't sure exactly what horrors she was expecting, but she knew that nothing wasn't one of them. Everything was fine. *Huh.* Weirdly enough, things were better than fine, which oddly didn't make her feel any better. Normally there would have been at least a couple of the furry creatures scurrying around.

She turned back toward the hallway that would lead her out of this place. She should leave and check out a couple of other trash receptacles to be sure, but she was now feeling more relaxed.

Oh yeah, droppings. She may as well poke around and find some droppings to test since this is the receptacle nearest the earlier disturbance.

Only, as she turned back, she caught movement out of the corner of her eye. She did a double take and her heart started to race. Over in the corner were about a dozen giant rats.

They were huddled together, but not for warmth. The space station was kept a constant temperature. Why were they together? And why were there so many of them? And why in stars name were they just staring at her.

What they should be doing is scurrying around looking for food. Or at least scurrying away at her presence. But in the last minute or so, none of them had moved. It was unnerving.

They continued to look at her and not move. It felt like they were waiting for something.

Floyd was right, these rats were huge, probably thirty to forty pounds each. She stayed frozen for a moment, trying to think of what to do. There were clear, fresh, rat droppings only a couple of feet away. It just happened that it was a couple of feet toward the rats themselves, which were maybe six or seven feet away. Seemed risky, but so far they were only standing there.

She held her breath and took a step. And then another one. None of them moved. She took out her baton and extended it. If one of them did decide to run over here while she was collecting the droppings, she could always push it back. And so, with one eye on the rat horde and another on the floor, she got what she needed. She put the container back in her pocket, but kept out the baton.

Then she backed away keeping an eye on them, but as it turned out, they never moved. In fact, it looked like all of their eyes were glazed over. She was starting to suspect by their strange behavior that they might be diseased after all. The priority now was getting back to her office, running the tests, and keeping Floyd in the loop. And more weapons. She was going to need more weapons. Not because they had done anything that was actually threatening, but because of her growing unease with the whole situation. She wasn't one to spook easy, and she always trusted her gut when it came to situations that didn't add up. With that thought she began a very fast sprint down the hallway past the wonky light. She didn't even slow down when she passed Carl and the Frenzy.

~

Maura found herself in her office filling out paperwork describing the earlier craziness. Now that it was over, it seemed like an even smaller ordeal than it had at the time. She couldn't believe how worked up she had gotten.

She chuckled to herself, took a sip of coffee, and looked the forms over. *Hmm.* She wondered about the whole Frenzy aspect.

A rat starting a bar fight? She began to wonder if they had gotten carried away just like she had. Either way it would probably be an entertaining story. She decided she'd drop the samples she had taken off at the lab, and then go to the Frenzy. The extra work wasn't required, specifically, but the paperwork she would turn in would look even better with an eyewitness interview.

The march across the station itself was always fun. Even though a few thousand permanent residents sounded like a lot, she usually saw at least a few familiar faces in the crowd.

Dropping off the samples was easy. Now she just had to make her way to the Frenzy. It had been a while since she'd visited as a patron, opting lately for some of the quieter bars that were closer to her apartment. Celestica seemed even busier than usual today as she walked across it.

Oh, look, a new restaurant. She stopped. The sign said: I, Pizza. *Ok*, thought Maura, *bonus points for a good name.* She stared in the window for a moment and decided that the patrons looked more than happy enough gobbling down their thin style pieces. She decided to come back soon to try it. She continued on.

Several minutes later, she approached the Frenzy. She paused, eyeing the doorman, who was a werewolf. A shaggy, tan one dressed in jeans and a t-shirt. She waited in line for a few minutes. When she got to the front, she squinted at the nametag and then smiled.

He smiled a jagged, toothy, carnivorous smile back at her. Then he looked over her clothes and squinted. It was a judgy, *you aren't dressed for the Frenzy* squint. Or maybe it was all in her head.

"Um, hello Carl, I'm Maura."

"Hello." He grinned in the trademark friendly manner of the Frenzy doormen. He still looked dubious about her, but apparently had made a decision to keep the line moving instead of making a big deal about it. "Fun and Frenzy await you, my lady."

"Sometimes," she answered him, "but right now I'm on duty."

He raised an eyebrow.

"I am in charge of pest control on the station. And I was hoping to interview some witnesses from the earlier rat incident. Employees, if possible." Her thought process was that the employees were less likely to be incapacitated, hopefully, seeing as they were on duty. And she didn't mention the fact that the rat was involved in a scuffle because she didn't want to put words in the mouth of any potential witnesses.

"Oh yeah," he said, his face brightening. "That was wild. How many witnesses do you need? Most of the employees there at the time are either gone or have been drinking wildly since then. Hold on a minute." He let the next few people in before turning back to her.

"So you were there?"

"I saw the whole thing," he answered. "I got here early before my shift and was kicking back at the bar."

"Drinking?"

"Nope," he said, "against company policy before a shift."

"Sorry," Maura said and pointed at the notepad in her hand, "I had to ask."

"No problem," he said. "Happy to help. But if you want to do this now, I have to clear it with my manager." He texted on his phone.

Maura stood to the side and watched him let in all of the patrons. A few minutes later, a lizard wearing a camo leisure suit came out.

"What's going on?" he asked.

"Larry, Maura," Carl said. "Maura, Larry. My boss. Hey, Larry. She needs to interview a sober employee who was here at the time of the, uh, rat incident."

Maura stood and switched her weight from foot to foot.

Larry looked thoughtful for a minute. "Well, kid, if that's what she's looking for, then it's a subset of exactly one."

All three of them stood there looking awkward for a moment.

"Oh, you need to do this now?" Larry asked.

"That would be very helpful," Maura replied, pointing to the notepad in her hand seriously, "the Celestica lawyer is all over me on this one. You don't see this every day."

"Now that's true," Larry said. "I wish I had seen it myself, I think the tales are getting taller in there every five minutes," he said, pointing to the bar. "Okay, you two can use my office around the corner, it's nice and quiet. I'll cover you, Carl, but the night shift is coming in soon, so make it snappy."

Maura thanked him and followed Carl around the corner to the office. When they entered, it looked more like a supply closet overflow than an actual working office. An ancient computer was gathering dust on an undersized desk piled high with old papers. Luckily, the only thing that mattered was that there were two old, metal, and extremely uncomfortable chairs. That would have to do. They sat down.

Maura got her notepad and paper ready again. She was recording the interview on her phone, of course, but it looked more professional to carry around good old fashioned paper and pencil.

"Let's start over," she said, "you said you were there, at the Frenzy nightclub, during the event in question at approximately two forty-seven that afternoon, right?" Maura nodded at him and waited for him to continue.

"Ok, yes," he said. "Like I said, I arrived early for my shift, and was just kicking back inside. Well, there were a bunch of rowdies on the end, way over in the corner where they always sit. Orcs, you know. They're surprisingly good tippers, by the way, orcs."

"You don't say."

"Actually, it had been an oddly quiet day up to that point. Isn't that the way it always is? The calm before the storm and all that."

"Tell me about it," Maura agreed. "Then what happened?"

"Well, I don't know exactly what happened before the shouting began. That's when I turned around and saw it."

"What did you see?" Maura asked. It was so hard not jumping the gun.

"I saw that mutant rat, that's what."

"The rat? So, you saw it. Was it really that big? And how in the name of stars did it start a bar fight?" Oh well, so much for not leading the witness.

Carl laughed. "These things do tend to take on a life of their own, don't they? Well, all I know is that I heard the yelling and I turned around. When I saw it, I assumed somebody had let a dog in here or something, although I could tell right away it was wild. Sort of."

Maura frowned. How could something look sort of wild? "What do you mean?"

"Well, when I saw it, it was circling the table in the back. The one with the rowdies, and they were freaking out, man. Half of the screams after that were because of the giant rat, and the other half of the screams were from the impressive number of illegal weapons that those guys pulled out upon seeing the rat. Once the screaming started, then everything happened really fast."

"What happened really fast?"

"The rat was circling the rowdies. And then it just stopped, like it was playing some weird game of duck-duck-goose. And those guys were yelling. And it's not like those orcs are easily spooked. But like I said, it was circling, and then it stopped. Then it bit the guy who happened to be sitting where it stopped."

"What?" Maura thought back to the phone call with Floyd over and over in her head and could clearly remember the notes she took. There was nothing in their conversation about anyone getting bit. She was pretty sure he would have mentioned that first.

She leaned forward in her chair. It creaked a metallic sound. "I'm sorry, are you telling me that not only did this rat bite someone, which wasn't in the information I received by the way, but that it, um, picked him?"

"Yes and yes." He smiled and nodded enthusiastically. "I was paying attention by then. That rat stopped right in front of that one orc, lunged forward and bit him. And that's not even the weird part."

Maura swallowed and wondered how the story could possibly get any stranger.

"After biting the guy, the rat ran right to a point in the middle of the room. It seemed to do it on purpose. It just stood there in the epicenter of all of the illegal weapons that were pulled. And then it, well, like, started dancing or something. Weirdest thing I've ever seen. Still can't seem to get the image of it out of my head."

Maura tried to sum up. "So, you're saying this rat came out of nowhere and chose a victim. Then, when it had attracted the entire room's attention, it went to the exact spot that would guarantee its own annihilation and then danced?"

"Yup."

"Until they all shot it dead."

"Yes. But not before those morons all shot each other. Duh. If everybody shoots at something in the middle of a circle then people and not just rats are going to get shot. That's what the hospital guy said."

"Who?"

"The hospital guy. Dr. Grayson. Always in here. Usually he's the one starting bar fights, sneaky bastard. This time it wasn't him though, but the outcome was the same. He comes in, patients for the hospital come out."

Maura frowned. "If Grayson wanted the maximum number of patients to go to the hospital, why didn't he grab the bite victim as he and the hospital staff were leaving?"

Carl shrugged. "No idea. The whole thing happened so fast. Maybe Grayson didn't see the bite, he was at the bar. He just came out afterward and took control of the aftermath. He called the hospital and coordinated everything."

"All of the victims of the idiot gun battle went to the hospital, right? What about the guy who got bit? Why didn't the lawyer mention him?"

Carl just shrugged. "Who knows? Orcs aren't always big fans of hospitals."

Maura thought about this. The whole thing was getting weirder and weirder. "Thanks, Carl," she said. "Oh, yeah, one more thing. Did you get the name of the guy who got bit? I want to check on him. You see, the lab is running a bunch of tests now, to see if there's any kind of sickness associated with this different breed of rat." She tried not to use the word disease with civilians per Floyd's standing instructions, although in reality it was a pointless endeavor.

She knew that was immediately where everybody's mind went. "If he does need treatment, I want to make sure that he gets it right away."

"I guess that makes sense," Carl said. "The guy who got bit is a regular. He's on the fringes of the rowdies, but mostly he keeps to himself."

"Name?" Maura asked again. "Somebody's got to go check on him, Carl."

"Steve. Steve from star station maintenance. Can't miss him. Big guy, black beard, ponytail."

"Steve from star station maintenance," Maura repeated out loud. She wrote it down for good measure. "Ok, thanks, Carl. You've been very helpful."

Maura walked out of the broom closet that doubled as Larry's office at the Frenzy and back out into the rest of the space station.

She took a deep breath and looked at all of the nice, normal people walking around. In hindsight, it felt like Carl had told her a ghost story. That would be fine, if it weren't her that had to do all of the follow up. Plus, she couldn't get the image of those creepy, giant rats huddled together just staring at her out of her head.

Her phone made a funny phaser sound effect. She checked it.

Get to work, you.

Hmmmm. That's new. It was from an S and M Motivation Corporation. That did sound familiar. Then she remembered an email about it. It was some new station wide productivity enhancement feature. Either Space Station Management was stupid, or it was just unaware of the seedy pun in the name. If Maura had to guess it would probably be option one.

I am working. I'm tracking down that orc rat bite victim. Please be ok, please be ok.

She made her way over toward starship maintenance to see if she could catch him. As it turned out, he was easier to catch than she thought.

"There he is," the shift manager said, as he pointed to a figure sitting motionless against the wall and staring into space.

"Um, is he on duty?" Maura asked. She was hoping that sitting there staring into space was normal.

"Supposed to be, but he reported for duty like that an hour ago. We asked him if he was okay, if he needed any help, but he just sat there."

Maura swallowed. "Is he normally that, um, quiet?"

"No. That's not normal. I heard he was in that rat bar fight, figure he had a few too many and needed to sleep it off. And that's very unusual, Steve has never had any problems holding his liquor."

"You said sleep it off," Maura said. She knelt down and waved a hand in front of Steve's face. "But he's not actually sleeping."

"You're right," he said, "I hadn't noticed. It gets very busy around here and I'm covering for Steve." Something beeped nearby. The shift manager moved on.

Maura was left with the catatonic looking Steve. She knew that hung over was not the same thing as unresponsive. *Weird.*

"Steve? I have reason to believe that you were injured yesterday. Is it okay if I check you over a little bit?"

Since he wasn't objecting, she looked over his jeans to see any evidence of a bite or wound or rip in the fabric. She found it right away. *Ouch.* The wound was angry and gaping. At the very least, he'd need stitches. And it still didn't explain why he was unresponsive. She decided to try again.

"Steve, can you hear me? My name is Maura. You're hurt, so I'm going to call the hospital and tell them to come and get you, okay? I have a doctor friend, there. She's the best. They will have you fixed up in no time. Ok?"

She stared at him for a moment. He was breathing and blinking and staring. *Huh.* She dialed the phone and called it in. Taking no chances, she also told them who she was and the background of the patient vis-à-vis the rat bar fight and the possibility of disease contamination, depending on the outcome of the tests. Then she hung up.

"Okay, Steve. They're coming, and they're going to take good care of you, okay?"

Maura shook her head and wondered if she should give Lyra a call. She decided to let them come get Steve first. Once he was taken care of, she could finish up some of this paperwork, give Floyd a heads up, and then maybe go visit Steve in the hospital. With any luck, all of this was just a series of weird coincidences.

~

Emily saw the orc being hovered into the Emergency Room waiting area. "I got him," she told Gorb, who bobbed at her in response.

"What have we got?" she asked as she looked down at the orc, who looked in reasonably good shape despite whatever ailment had brought him in here. In fact, he looked quite peaceful, so peaceful she wondered what the EMTs had given him. And if they had any more. "Hey, what meds did you give this guy? He looks totally strung out. Or are we looking at some new exotic drug making its way around the station?"

"We didn't give him anything, didn't have to," the EMTs said as they walked alongside her toward the patient rooms. "As to what he's on, we have no idea. Maura called us, you know the pest control girl? Well, she said that he's a rat bite victim that fell through the cracks at the Frenzy. See?"

He pointed to the patient's leg. The patient's jeans were ripped and he had a gash in his leg.

Emily stopped walking. "I'm sorry, did you say that this was a rat bite?"

"That's what we were told."

She hurried to catch back up to the patient, mind swimming with all of the unpleasant fears that her earlier rat necropsy has brought up. But this was just a poor orc who got bit by the evil thing. And then, what? Maybe self-medicated. It wasn't fully adding up. "Why wasn't he brought in with the rest of the Frenzy patients?"

"You're asking the wrong guys," they said. "Who was in charge at the Frenzy in the first place?"

"Grayson," Emily muttered. "Figures. Put him in Operating Room five."

You've got this, Emily. Just fix this guy up and then the next time you run into Grayson you can ask him how he managed to let a rat bit victim leave the scene of a major incident.

"Hello, Steve, I'm going to clean this wound, ok?"

He hadn't said anything since they brought him in, but sometimes people were scared. Or on something. She smiled at him. Nothing. She waved a hand in front of his face. Nothing.

"Alright, I'm still going to give you a little bit of pain medicine because I don't know what's going on with you or what you've taken. Like I said, I'm going to clean this wound and get you some antibiotics. And probably some shot that Disease Control deems necessary, I'm going to have to look that up a little later, but first things first."

The wound wasn't so bad. It cleaned up and stitched up pretty quickly, especially with the lack of chatter. Despite his lack of conversation and consciousness, the rest of his vital signs were fine. The patient was acting off, though. Weirdly detached and unresponsive. She waved a hand in front of his face just to see what would happen. Nothing, not even a snarky comment. And that was very unusual here, these residents had a comeback for everything.

She was finishing up when a thought struck her. The rat. It had severe brain abnormalities. What if that was some disease that it had. What if it could pass that onto an orc patient? *No,* she thought. *That would be crazy.*

Still, a quick brain scan wasn't a bad idea, especially since if he was on a new drug that they would have to track in the future, it would help to get a readout on that as well.

She grabbed the pen like device and took a breath. She pointed it at his forehead and pushed the button. *Here goes nothing.* Beep.

She looked at the readout. Then she hyperventilated again. Then she wasn't sure exactly what to do. This guy's brainwave activity was also off the charts, and it was in the ballpark of the dead mutant rat.

14

Lyra had to hurry, but she did manage to beat Vax to the room where his patient had somehow deteriorated and set off an emergency notification. *Ha.* The two of them had a sort of competition going on, although now that she thought about it, he probably didn't even know.

Of course, she had already been in this room a couple of times and heard Vax and Nancy talking about this particular patient, but she had only gotten snippets. In hindsight, the snippets she had gotten were weird. It wasn't her fault, though, she had been distracted by the rat.

The minute she ducked into the room, though, the strangeness of the whole thing washed over her. The hairs on her arms and neck stood up.

The patient was sitting up, which should have been good except for a couple of details. One, it was her understanding that this particular patient had been in a coma since arriving and shouldn't necessarily be sitting up. And for sure he shouldn't be singing.

And it wasn't any normal kind of singing, not any kind she had ever heard of, anyway. It was more a weird kind of emotionless, tuneless, vocalizing that didn't involve any lip movement at all. Lyra could not possibly imagine walking into a creepier situation.

But there he was, right in front of her, sort of singing. While sitting up, and with his eyes huge and fixed.

Swallowing hard and unsure of what to expect, she approached the patient cautiously, grabbing the flashlight out of her coat pocket. She fixed the beam of light on one of the patient's pupils and then the other and got the exact same response. Nothing. She checked again and got the same reaction. Where the hell was Vax, anyway? She briefly considered ducking out of the room and pretending she was never there. *Get it together, Lyra.*

She checked all of the patient's vital statistics on the readouts and tried to see a pattern, the only pattern was that everything appeared completely normal.

Except for the Patient Emergency Notification she had received, of course, which appeared to be because the brain waves of the singing patient appeared to have flatlined sometime in the last twenty minutes. She double checked everything again and realized that none of it made sense. She hadn't felt this way since medical school, when an idiot attending had decided to pull pranks on her.

She sighed hoping that Vax was indeed pulling a prank, but the hairs on the back of her neck said otherwise.

A noise startled her and she jumped, but it was only a phone notification. It was from Arthur. He found the manual for MACRO. *Good for him.* She took a couple of deep breaths and tried to steady herself.

Then she did the only thing she could think of, and crossed the room to grab the chart, keeping a wary eye on the patient. She decided that from now on she'd just let Vax beat her to these P.E.N notifications. At least some of the time.

In fact, she was still standing there pretending to look at the chart when Vax finally crashed into the room, almost literally. He gave her a dirty look and then noticed the patient was sitting up. Lyra rolled her eyes at the order of events.

"What the-" he said.

"Good news," Lyra deadpanned, "your patient is awake. Now would you mind telling me what in stars name is going on here? I thought he was in a coma."

The patient stopped the weird vocalizing for a moment and there was nothing but dead silence in the room. If anything, it was creepier than the singing. The patient was only pausing though. He took a long, wheezing breath and then started again. It was like nails on a chalkboard of all of her musical senses.

"How long's he been like this?" Vax asked just as Nancy entered the room. Nancy was breathless from running and stopped suddenly upon entering. She took one look at the patient and took a few steps back. "Lyra, what did you do to him?"

"Easy," Lyra said. "I didn't do anything except foolishly beat you guys to your creepy patient. What the hell. You really should give people a heads up if your work descends into b-movie weirdness." Then Lyra remembered Gorb and Grayson and all the other nosy people who loved to lurk around hospital hallways.

"Hey, guys, what do you say we close the door until we figure out what in stars name is going on here before letting every doctor and passerby duck in here and gawk?"

Nancy recovered herself and closed the door.

Vax repeated his question. "How long has he been like this?"

"You mean sitting up with fixed and dilated pupils and doing this weird vocalizing/singing thing? No idea. I got here just before you. Which parts of this was he not doing before?"

"All of it," Nancy said.

Nancy joined Vax in looking over the equipment and double checking the numbers. "Usually, brain wave function flat-lining does not accompany sitting up and singing or whatever that is."

Nancy walked over to the patient and waved a hand in front of his eyes with no response.

Vax pulled out his flashlight and examined the pupils, as Lyra had done earlier. She sat and watched.

"Did you get the same response with the flashlight that I did?" Lyra asked.

"I don't know," Vax answered, "what response did you get?"

"Nothing."

"Then yes. I got the same response. Twice."

Lyra wasn't sure what to do next. "I think it's safe to say that we're in uncharted territory here. The important question is, what do we do next? Or who do we call."

"You want to call Grayson."

"I don't know," Lyra said, "I've never seen anything like it, but the whole thing is starting to feel like it's way above my pay grade."

Vax crossed his arms. "You're just the teacher's pet."

"Yeah, that's me," Lyra deadpanned, "always kissing up to Grayson. Look, if you have any other ideas, I'm listening."

She crossed her arms, making sure she kept both Nancy and Vax between her and the patient. She wondered why she was doing that. It was almost like it was some kind of reflex. Why in space would she be afraid of a barely conscious patient with no brainwave activity? She waited, secretly hoping that Vax would figure out what was going on and make her feel better about the whole situation. The singing continued.

"Wait," Lyra said, re-checking the brainwave info. "When I got here, it was because the brain wave function had plummeted, right?"

"Yes, that appears to be the case," Vax said.

"Well, it's not anymore. According to these new numbers, not only is there brain function, it's unbelievable. It's like he's a genius on red bull."

A cell message from Ian broke the silence. He was very

excited about something. Something about the numbers he was studying jumping around just a few minutes ago. Or at least that was the gist of it that she got while skimming and being stared at in awkward silence by Vax and Nancy.

Um. Yay. I'm a little busy right now, though. In the middle of an emergency code. Will talk later.

When she looked up Vax and Nancy were staring at her. "What?" Lyra asked at last.

"Are we interrupting you?" Vax asked.

Lyra felt her cheeks get hot. Of course, the texts. "Was I interrupting you guys? It's not like you were actually doing anything or had any ideas. Speaking of which, what exactly are we going to do?"

She started humming, then caught herself, realizing that she was actually joining in with the patient. The stares continued in her direction.

"And what's with your patient and that weird singing type noise he's making? And the whole eyeball thing." Lyra took a step toward Vax, pointing a finger up at his chest. "You have bigger problems than me getting a text message, mister. This is your patient. You should be the one figuring out what to do."

"Okay," he said, looking as panicked as she had ever seen him. "You're right. Let's think it through. Maybe he did regain consciousness. And what if he's just blind? He was unconscious when he was brought in, so there's no way for us to know what condition he was in before he got here."

Okay, that actually made sense. And it helped Lyra feel a little better. Maybe this simply wasn't as strange as it appeared to be.

That's when the patient turned his head to look right at Lyra. She screamed and backed into Nancy, who also started screaming.

Lyra's blood ran cold with those eyes staring right through her soul. Despite the pupils being huge and unreactive, she could swear he was looking at her on purpose.

Vax just stood there with his mouth open. Then he drew his sword. Lyra wasn't sure whether he was planning on using it to think, as usual, to defend himself and Nancy, or to kill the patient. He looked pretty freaked out.

Just when Lyra was sure that the singing noise the patient was making was the creepiest thing in the entire universe, the patient stopped. He took another long, deep, ragged breath and started again. This time it was louder, at a higher octave, and had a desperate, ominous tone to it. In other words, even worse than before.

Lyra, Vax, and Nancy covered their ears with their hands. Lyra got another set of texts from Ian. *Are you kidding me with this*? She wanted to take out all of her current frustration on him, but halted, fingers poised over the phone keyboard, when she read his text.

Numbers went even crazier again. What in stars name is going on tonight? Hope your crisis is going okay.

Lyra frowned. Indeed. What was going on tonight? Was there any chance at all that the incidents could be connected? Ian obviously had nothing to do with the weird, singing, brain-dead to genius output medical mystery patient, but something was obviously going on. What if there were other weird things happening here on the station that were connected? One, it was all she had to go on right now, and two, she'd be willing to run down almost any lead no matter how crazy in order to get out of this particular room.

"Hey, guys?" Lyra asked, texting Ian back a question that was nagging her.

"Do you think now is really the time for us to be dealing with your relationship issues?" Vax asked.

Lyra shot him a dirty look and tried and failed to ignore the comment. "Yes, this has to do with my date tonight. You should try dating. It would probably improve your mood and your bedside manner. Anyway, my date tonight, Ian is a scientist, you see. And he said that the algorithm experiment he was working on went all haywire, just now."

Vax crossed his arms. "So?"

Lyra ignored him as she received another text from Ian. She skimmed it and then turned her attention back to Vax. "You see, his experiment went all wonky exactly twice tonight. The first anomaly seems to line up timewise with the new song here from top forty radio patient, and the other one coincides with the exact minute that we all got the Patient Emergency Notification a little while ago."

"That is weird." Nancy looked dubious, but interested. "It couldn't possibly be connected though, right? How could it?"

"I don't know," Lyra answered. "But what if it's not just us, not just the patient. What if something is going wonky right now on the space station itself? What if it's affecting more than just us?"

"Seems like a long shot," Vax said.

Lyra knew he was right. She also knew she was going to get the hell out of this room now. "I know it's a long shot, but since there's no other working theories right now, I'm going to check it out."

She texted Ian that she'd meet him at a coffee shop that was approximately halfway between his apartment and the hospital and headed out. "You guys text me if you figure anything out in the meantime," she called over her shoulder.

~

Gorb doodled in a notepad he pulled out of his desk drawer. A doctor came in and called the next patient. He looked up before turning back to his doodling. Already behind on his paperwork, he was avoiding it. All of the cases so far this morning had been so boring.

A tune played in the back of his head. A strange tune that was not familiar to him. At least not that he could remember. It seemed to come and go in his head and he found that his ideas about it had made their way into his doodle.

Instead of the usual boxes and waves that he usually drew, there were quite a bit of circles. Which was funny, because circles were hard to draw with tendrils and were his least favorite.

It seemed to him, thinking back, that every once in a while, he could hear one of the patients singing, but he couldn't be sure. He stopped doodling for a minute to listen, but right now there was only silence, so he couldn't confirm his theory.

He went and got a cup of coffee and brought it back to his desk. Then he stared at it. He couldn't drink it, of course, he was a jellyfish. But he liked the way the liquid sloshed in the cup, and he liked carrying it around like he was important. *Look at me with my coffee.*

He swished back and forth and took stock of the waiting room. There had been a dozen patients today, give or take.

He grabbed a pen and began his morning ritual of trying to find a way to balance it where his ear would be if he had one. He had just begun when the odd singing started again. The same strange song he had been hearing on and off, even when he wasn't paying attention.

He tried to place the tune. There was something familiar about it, but he still couldn't place it. He drifted up the hallway to confirm that the sound was coming from a patient room. *Yup.*

Satisfied, he went back to his desk. *Whew, there's that mystery solved.* He grabbed the pen again and started to concentrate.

Blaring alarms and red flashing lights lit up the room. These particular warning lights were rare, signaling a space station-wide emergency.

Gorb loved the adrenaline of these moments and it always seemed to him like the place turned into a magical disco. That was, except for all of the shouting and running and stuff.

Lyra came running in. "Hi, Gorb."

"It wasn't me, this time," Gorb said, holding innocent tendrils in the air for her to see.

Lyra didn't pay any attention to him, though and continued running past him down the hall.

Gorb drifted down the hall to see what she was doing, which he could, because he could propel himself around without making any noise whatsoever, which usually allowed him to hear all kinds of juicy information.

This time he drifted just close enough to not be noticed. That was the room with the patient that had been taken in while being pursued.

Gorb remembered. The excitement from it had not died down yet, not by a long shot. Sure, the hornet EMT had recovered well and had left in a day, but the other guy.

Well, Vax and Nancy were spending more and more time in there trying to figure out why the guy wasn't recovering properly. And they weren't in there just doing the usual hanky panky either. It seemed to have something to so with brain waves, but Gorb couldn't be sure.

Gorb couldn't hear anything interesting from the room with Lyra in it, so he drifted back to his desk, continuing to think of all the weird recent events.

And then there was the whole rat thing, he thought. Gorb hadn't been invited to the upper level management emergency meeting, of course, but he had heard about it. And the rat bar fight. And the possible quarantine.

He smiled. Sort of. Not a smile that a non-jellyfish would notice, but it was there just the same. That's right, nothing happened in this hospital that he didn't know about. He prided himself on his nosiness.

The alarms and flashing lights turned off, presumably because Lyra was there fixing whatever it was that needed to be fixed.

He looked around the waiting room. All of the patients seemed to go back to being occupied by their phones or books.

Vax came running around the corner too. "Hi, Vax." He didn't say anything, though, he just went to join Lyra.

Gorb was just about to leave to go eavesdrop again when he heard a whirring sound behind him.

"Oh hello," Gorb said. "Who are you? Are you that kooky robot that they talk about? The one that hangs out in the doctor's lounge even though you're not a doctor?"

The robot was adorable. He was silver with a blue fin on his head. Gorb liked him. He was beeping like crazy, and also going around in circles.

"Beep boop to you too!" Gorb shimmied back and forth in time with the robot's circles. A person ambled up to the counter. "Hello? I'm here to check in?"

"In a minute," Gorb said, "can't you see that I'm busy?"

"You're dancing with a robot," the guy said.

Gorb didn't like his tone, and he didn't look all that sick. In fact, Gorb was torn between a comment and a threat to sting the guy for interrupting when Lyra went running by again. That's when he remembered that he had meant to go eavesdrop.

"Hey, Lyra!" he called, "where ya going? Look! I made a new robot friend. This little guy is adorable, isn't he? He's all beep boop boop."

"Sorry, Gorb," she said, blowing past. "I have to go. In the middle of a crisis. You know me."

"But he's really cute," Gorb called out. "Look, he rolls around in circles, and his little antenna keeps blinking red. I think that means he likes me."

Lyra stopped and came back. Her eyes flicked from Gorb to the robot and then stayed there.

"Isn't he cute?" Gorb repeated.

"Gorb," she said, her face scrunched up into an adorable frown. "How long's he been doing that?"

Gorb did his best to shrug, but it didn't work. Probably because he didn't have shoulders. "I don't know. Maybe twenty minutes? Hey, what's the big crisis, can I help?"

"Oh yeah, Ian," Lyra said. "Sorry, Gorb. I have to go right now, but I'm going to come back, ok? You keep MACRO here. I have some questions for him when I get back."

"What's a *Macro*?" Gorb asked.

"The robot's name is MACRO."

"Ok!" Gorb waved a tendril at her, but she speed-walked out the door. "Bye, Lyra!"

15

Lyra walked quickly toward the coffee shop where she was meeting Ian wondering what the deal was with MACRO. She had never seen him act that way before. Not with the circles, and not with that tone or frequency of beeping.

She had to admit that most of this new theory of hers was simply an excuse to sneak out of that patient room, not that she believed that there was actually a connection. But what were the odds that Ian's issues would line up with the weird patient's timeline or that MACRO picked this exact moment to go crazy?

She wanted to get the robot manual and do some more investigating, but she knew she didn't have time right now. Things were getting serious. One mystery at a time. Then it hit her. *Arthur.*

She forced herself to slow down so she could text him.

Remember our secret project? Grab manual, go to emergency room waiting area desk and figure out what in the name of our black hole he's trying to communicate. This is a priority. Text me when you know anything. Please.

There. That done, she walked faster in order to find Ian. If nothing else today, she was getting her exercise. She was further toward the coffee shop than she thought however, and by the time she finished her text and lurched forward she nearly ran headlong right into Ian.

The two collided.

"Lyra? You okay? You look like you've seen a ghost." He chuckled.

"Great," she said, "and here I was thinking I was doing a good job of hiding it."

Ian's expression changed. "You mean you *did* see a ghost? What's going on at that hospital, anyway?"

"No, no," Lyra said, trying to catch her breath. "No ghosts. Not exactly. But I am interested in finding out more about what is going on with your research tonight."

"You really came all the way here to meet me in the middle of your crisis to ask me about my project?"

"Well, it's more like Vax's crisis than mine," she said. *That was the whole point of sneaking out of the room earlier.*

Lyra could see by his face that he was starting to seriously wonder what was going on. And she didn't blame him. She also wasn't exactly sure where she should start. Or how much to tell him. The last thing she wanted to do was to cause a panic. She didn't even know exactly what it was that she didn't want people to panic about.

She took a few deep breaths and suggested that they keep going to the coffee house they were originally supposed to meet at.

He nodded and led the way. At least that gave her a plan and a few minutes to think about what she was going to say and how she was going to say it. And if her hunch was right, and something weird was going on, then some caffeine wouldn't be a bad idea anyway.

They ordered their individual coffee drinks in a surreal moment of normalcy.

Strange things were afoot, she could feel it coming, she just didn't know exactly what to do about it or how to stop it. Maybe Ian could help. Maybe he would just leave thinking she was crazy. Only one way to find out. They found a table in the back that offered a little bit of privacy and sat down.

"Thanks for the coffee, Ian."

"Any time. Although, and please don't take this as a criticism, you already look a little stressed out, and I'm not sure that a double shot of expresso was the best idea." He held his hands up in a sign of surrender, upon seeing her eyes narrow at him. "But I'd also like to say that whatever this thing is, I'm in. And if this thing is going to keep us up really, really, late, and I hope it does," he stopped to wink at her, "then I want you to know I'm extra in. One hundred percent. Lay it on me."

Lyra thought through the possibilities of what to say to him and then winked back at him. Then she whispered. "Okay, but no takebacks, because this is going to get really weird."

Lyra wasn't at all sure that Ian was ready to hear what she had to say, no matter how eager he seemed. She took a gulp of expresso for courage before beginning.

Ian raised an eyebrow. "I want to hear all about this medical weirdness. I think. But if that's what this is about. And I guess it is because we're whispering now. Then why in the name of your black hole would you be the least bit interested in my research?"

Excellent intro, Lyra thought, *I'll start there*. "Because you texted it to me."

He looked more confused. She took a sip of expresso.

"Okay," she started again. "You see, there's this patient who's acting very strangely. He had no brainwave activity briefly, so technically you could say he was dead. Except that later he was sitting up and singing and at one point appeared to respond to stimuli."

The stimuli in question being me, she thought. She repressed a shudder and decided that last part was better left out.

Ian's face went a shade of white that Lyra found fitting for the turn in the conversation.

"You're saying you have some sort of zombie patient?" He scooted his chair slightly away from her. It made a skidding noise and she gave him a sharp look. "Sorry. Um, but do you mind if I ask if the whole zombie thing is catchy? Because I've seen a bunch of these movies and they never, ever, end well."

Lyra opened and closed her mouth. She hadn't even thought about it. *Zombie patient?* To be fair, it had been a very odd night, but probably not zombie apocalypse odd. "I don't think he's a zombie."

"Why not?"

"Well one, because there's no such thing as actual zombies. It's not in medical terminology at all. For a reason. Sure, there are rumors, but I've certainly never seen anything to believe that any of that stuff was real."

"Until tonight," he countered.

"Pretty sure it's not a zombie. Can we stop talking about zombies? I mean, if we're worried about anything possibly being catchy, what we should be worried about is the oversized mutant rat that started the bar fight."

Ian's eyes got huge and that's when Lyra figured out that she had gotten off topic. And also, that she had already had way too much caffeine. She decided to stop talking for a minute. Except that she couldn't stop, because she had this horrible nagging feeling that bad things were happening right now, and she was running out of time. "Are you kidding me? You have to be the only person on Celestica who hasn't heard about that bar fight."

"Okay," he jumped in mercifully, "you do appear to have a lot on your mind tonight. There's the zombie patient zero and the mutant rat. Anything else?"

Rats, plural, she thought. Lyra decided to go ahead and tell him everything. If she had to deal with all of the crap thrown at her, then he could as well. Hopefully. She would consider this whole thing a test for him. "Oh yeah there's one more thing, the robot's gone crazy."

"What robot?"

"The one that hangs out in the doctor's lounge. He always seems to know when something is about to happen."

"Why does he hang out in the doctor's lounge? Is he a robot doctor?" He looked way too excited about the possibility.

"No, Ian. He's not a robot doctor." She ran her finger through her hair. "Look. I know that this is confusing and that you're trying very hard to keep up, but that's not what's important right now." Her cellphone buzzed. It was Vax. She skimmed. The patient was doing something weird and new.

"What's that?" Ian asked, probably seeing her expression change as she read the text.

"That's Vax, head of surgery. He said the patient is doing something else that's new and creepy."

"Like what?"

"I don't know, maybe his head is spinning around. Maybe he is a zombie." *Hold it together Lyra.*

Ian's phone buzzed also. He looked down at his phone and then back up at her.

"Ok, what's your news?" Lyra asked.

"Weird," he said. "My numbers just took another sideways leap."

"See?" Lyra asked. "That right there. That's why I asked you about your work," she said triumphantly as she realized that at long last she had finally gotten to her actual point. And it was true, as far-fetched as it might be, it was why she was right here right now.

He looked dubious.

"Because the texts you were sending me about your project turning in a new direction, well it seemed to correspond to when the patient was flat lining or altering his behavior. And I thought that maybe strange events were happening on the entire space station and not just to this one patient. I was hoping anyway, because then maybe it would be less weird. But now that I say it out loud, I don't believe that to be the case. Not at all."

She sat back and slumped her shoulders. Then, in an act of defiance against common sense and recent events, she slurped down the last of the double expresso. If she was going out tonight in a zombie apocalypse or whatever, at least she'd go out the way she lived. Wired.

Ian took a sip of his coffee too and seemed to consider this for a moment before metaphorically punting the ball back at her. "Don't you need to go check on that?" He indicated her phone and presumably the text from Vax. It was clear he didn't fully believe her.

"Ah, Vax can take care of himself," she said. "It's his patient, after all." Then she got an idea. "Hold on," she said, grabbing her phone. "Look, the first text you sent me came in just a few minutes after the initial Patient Emergency Notification that started the whole thing and sent me there tonight. Did you text me the minute the numbers went sideways or a few minutes afterward?"

"Well, I double checked everything first. I figured there was probably an error."

"Exactly. And this last text came through only seconds after the change in patient behavior in the hospital room. I was there and saw the whole thing. What about the next time, was there a delay?"

Ian shook his head. "I see where you're going, and it does seem like a very unlikely coincidence. I just don't see how my research and your zombie could possibly be connected."

Ian had raised his voice too much this time, and there were a few startled expressions from people nearby. It didn't help that she was in her medical coat and that both of them looked worried and were whispering.

"Book club," Lyra announced loudly, "it's okay, folks." She tried to diffuse the situation, but they weren't buying it. "We're talking about this weird book called The Mystery Patient, you should check it out."

Another text came though. This one was from Arthur. Something about MACRO. His text didn't make any sense though. She frowned at the phone. He was at the waiting room. As much as she hated to go back there, she knew that she had to. That's where everything was happening.

Then she got an idea. "Hey, do you have any portable equipment? For your project? I'm asking because maybe you can use your equipment to scan the patient, see if he's the one that's making your numbers all wonky. It's worth a try, right?"

Ian went all pale again, probably at the thought of getting close enough to scan the zombie patient. She rolled her eyes. "He's not really a zombie, okay? I've got an idea. How about if you show me how to work the equipment? I'll scan the zombie, and you can run the numbers."

He managed a weak smile. "You said zombie."

She smiled in response. "Fine, you're right. It's just more fun to say zombie."

He thought about it for a minute and then appeared to come to a decision. He stood up to leave. She couldn't help but feel a little bad, but she couldn't blame him. The whole thing was just too crazy.

"Well," he said to her after a pause, "let's go get my equipment. Are you coming or not?"

Lyra jumped up and followed him. They left the coffee shop and headed down the hallway. She looked around to make sure nobody was around. "I'd kiss you if you weren't so worried about being around me now that I treated patient zero in the zombie apocalypse," she teased.

She waited a moment and wondered if he had not heard her in all of the excitement, but then he stopped dead in his tracks and turned.

His face was flushed from running and excitement and caffeine. He was facing her, all tall and dark with the curly hair and the muscles. He leaned in. "Well, we all gotta go sometime, right?" he whispered in her ear.

"I wouldn't put you in any actual danger," she said, moving closer to him. "It's weird, but it's not zombie apocalypse weird, ok?"

"But it could be," he countered. "Is this your attempt to get one last p-d-a in before the end?" He smiled a smile so charming it would have turned into even more than a kiss if there weren't a full-blown crisis going on.

"Take it or leave it," she said, smiling back. Their lips met.

Lyra was lost in that moment until a catcall rang out down the hallway. Feeling a rush of heat to her face, she stepped back and smoothed out her white coat with her hands.

Either way, Ian had passed the test tonight. Even though he was visibly frightened of the zombie apocalypse, and she had had contact with the patient and the rat, he had still kissed her. He was in this now, right up to his eyeballs.

"Right," she said, pulling away, "back to the mystery."

Scythe made his way toward the main communications hub on the space station. He didn't need a map or directions, he could feel the energy, hear the voices as they translated through the ship. Following these signals was child's play to him.

This time, the residents seemed to steer clear of him quietly. And that was the last thing he had expected, for this place to be so weird already that he would fit in.

He arrived at and opened the door of the communications center. A handful of employees were scattered around playing phone games.

He shut the door, went to the center of the room, and raised his arms.

That's when the employees began to notice him. "Shit, what's with the mask, dude-" The man moved quickly and physically removed the mask from Scythe's face.

Scythe let him and then turned his face toward him.

Screaming sounded in the room, drowning out all other sounds, including the specific information that he was looking for.

A single finger aimed at each was enough to terminate them. The room went quiet again so that he could concentrate, gaining the knowledge of the specific target that he was interested in.

After a few moments, he stopped and he smiled. He found it. This target was everything he had ever dreamed about. Intelligent, brave, and utterly alive in every sense of the word. He practically salivated at the thought of the specimens he would be reaping soon, he wasn't just here for one soul, he just needed the one to focus on and the rest would be surplus. Yes, soon he would have all that he'd need. He also put out an electrical hit on anything that could possibly stand in his way. His victory was nigh.

He walked out of the communications room and into the hallway in a good mood, nearly running headlong into a guy with a goofy red hat.

"Hello, citizen of Celestica," he said, "I am Scythe. I am about to change your life. You see, I am here to free you." He leaned down toward the little man, waiting to see if for once somebody would take him up on his offer before their reality was altered. Alas, it wasn't to be. He ran off like he had seen a ghost. *Oh well.* These residents would belong to him soon enough.

16

"Hey, Dr. man, what are you doing to my friend?" Gorb asked.

He was clapping his tendrils together in an excited way. Or maybe a threatening way. Arthur wasn't sure which.

"I'm trying to communicate with MACRO here. Or at least understand him." He flipped through the pages of the manual. "I can't tell if he's agitated or just malfunctioning."

"He's fine," Gorb said, pointing. "Look at him. He's having fun. Actually, I think he's dancing. It's the music."

"What?" Arthur asked.

"The music. The radio. That's when he started getting his freak on. That's right, you're an awesome little freak," he said to MACRO. "Way cooler than the square doctor here."

MACRO continued to frantically beep, flash his red light in a sequence, and roll around in tight little circles. Then all of that stopped and for a moment he froze, emitting the absolutely ordinary single chirpy beep Arthur was used to. The one that meant that a new patient was incoming.

Arthur turned toward the landing bay just in time to see a gurney being hovered in. He turned back to MACRO for a moment and saw that he had gone back to his erratic behavior after correctly alerting him to the new patient. Maybe Lyra wasn't crazy at all when she suggested that he was trying to communicate something important to them. He put the manual down on Gorb's desk and turned back to the EMTs.

"What have we got?" he asked.

"Squid. Knife fight. Internal wounds."

Arthur froze for a moment. Then he blurted out, "Vax."

"Sorry, Vax is in with the weirdo patient," Gorb said.

"Lyra," Arthur suggested.

Gorb beamed. "She's gone too. Second date with the same guy tonight. Don't you call her. She's bus-y."

Arthur frowned. *How could Gorb possibly know that? Were Gorb and Lyra closer than he thought?* "We can page somebody, who's on call tonight?"

Gorb pretended to flip through an invisible book on his desk before looking up and sashaying playfully back and forth, causing a slight breeze. "That would be you, doctor man. You're the one on call."

Smartass. Shit, he was right. Arthur wiped his face with his hand. His heart raced. He tried to remember what Lyra had told him. She believed in him. *"You're worth taking a chance on,"* she had said. Lately, his fear of never being able to move forward was rivaling his fear of the inside of Cephalopods anyway. *Squishy, gross, tentacle-y cephalopods. Why'd it have to be a squid?* He looked around to see if there weren't more patients needing attention, maybe a nice, injured insectoid, but no such luck.

The paramedics and the patient had passed him now and were heading down the hallway toward a room. "Are you coming?" one of them called. "Or do you want us to treat him ourselves?"

Why is everybody in this hospital a smartass? His initial instinct was to pull out his phone and go over the major internal systems of that species again, but he knew them all by heart. In fact, he knew the information backwards and forwards and everything squishy in between. The only thing he lacked was actual experience.

The one other time he was actually in the room with a cephalopod patient, he had flat passed out. He only regained consciousness later with Grayson throwing water on him in the doctor's lounge.

"Coming," he called, but it was mostly because he had no choice and the horrible silence was getting to him. It was, above all, time to do his job.

"You can do it, Arthur. I believe in you." Gorb held up his little tendrils in loops that Arthur could only guess was supposed to be a thumbs-up gesture. "The robot believes in you too, look. He turned his circles the other way. I think that's what that means."

"MACRO."

"What?" Gorb asked, losing the thumb structure and returning to his normal shape.

"The robot's name is MACRO."

A nurse was calling him now and he had to go. As he walked down the hallway toward his and possibly the patient's doom, he heard Gorb loudly whisper to MACRO, "I can't believe he's going to do it."

Crash was having a busy day. His date for the evening bailed and he was three quarters of the way through the contacts on his phone trying to get another one. So far, no luck.

Then there were all of the incoming phone calls. Fires were popping up all over the station. Not actual fires, mind you, but it meant work for him just the same. The residents seemed needier than usual today.

His phone rang again. Crash listened. "Can you repeat that?" he asked, pressing record. A body. That was pretty unusual. The gatekeeper on duty had been found dead. Even stranger. "Okay," he said, "send all of the security footage to my computer."

Crash's computer chimed with the arrival of the footage. He ignored another phone call while he fast forwarded. When he saw the strange, masked, hooded figure appear he paused it.

"What the-"

That's when he knew he had a real problem. If this really was the killer, all he had to do was ditch the mask and hood and he could be anywhere on the space station. They wouldn't even know who they were looking for. That would make everything a lot more difficult.

He kept fast forwarding, hoping that this guy wasn't the killer. But it wasn't to be, the masked figure seemed to point at the gatekeeper and he just went down. Just like that. And then the masked figure left and the gatekeeper stayed. He wiped his face scales with his hands. *Oh boy, this is going to be a long day.* He was still contemplating putting a quiet APB out for this masked guy in hopes that he was dumb enough to keep his Halloween costume on when there was a knock on his door. He looked up just as he answered the ringing phone for the fourteenth time in the last hour. The phone fell out of his hand onto the desk.

"Hello?" It vibrated and chirped. "Hello, Crash? Are you there?"

Crash hung up the phone without taking his eyes off of the newcomer, who lurched into the room and heaved himself into the chair opposite Crash.

Crash couldn't help but stare at him. It was the figure from the security footage, mask and hood and all. *Unbelievable. What kind of nutcase am I dealing with here?* He decided to try to keep the situation calm for now. "Can I help you?"

"You're in charge of security, here, yes?" His voice had a metallic ring to it.

Crash couldn't help but notice the odd stiffness to his movements. And the strange mask. He had never seen one quite like it before. What exactly was it that he was looking at? It's not like he didn't run into his share of crazies as head of security on one of the universe's most distant space stations. He was still stumped, though. "Yes, that's me. I'm in charge of security. What exactly can I do for you?"

The stupid phone rang again. Crash didn't even remember placing it back on the receiver after the suspect walked into the room. He picked it up, mostly out of instinct and because of the uncomfortable silence since the newcomer failed to answer. He seemed stuck or something. Crash kept an eye on him, though, and decided to use the phone call as a distraction to reach under his desk and get the biggest BFG within current arms reach.

"Hello, what's the problem? Oh, it's you hospital people again. Noise complaint? About a patient? What kind of nonsense is this?" He held up his hands in a what are you gonna do gesture, in an effort to put the suspect at ease while his other hand felt around for the mini laser howitzer he always kept nearby. *Whew. Found it.*

"Well, why don't you just sedate him or call the shrink or something? You can't possibly be asking me to go down there and arrest an emergency room patient that arrived just yesterday."

Crash had seen that patient, and he was in bad shape. There was no way that guy was actually causing a disturbance. He wondered if there wasn't a gas leak or something over at the hospital. That was the only thing that could justify the number of phone calls he was getting. He hung up and scribbled a quick note to call environmental and get them to double check the area

before looking back up into the steel blue mask of the matter at hand.

The figure had located one of Crash's other numerous weapons around the room. "Don't touch that," Crash said, raising his weapon so the figure could see it.

Maybe it wasn't a great idea to randomly place weapons around his own office.

The figure slowly put the weapon back down again. "Trust me, I don't need your primitive, ineffective weapons."

You're about to figure out just how effective my weapons are, Crash thought.

The figure rose to his feet stiffly. "I am known as Scythe. And I'm here to set you free."

Crash didn't expect that. He expected to say, *look, I saw the security footage and know that you're a murder suspect*, but something told him to hold off. He ran a bunch of scenarios through his mind as to what he could possibly mean. *Is he hitting on me? What's going on here?* "Scythe, you say? Is that a first or a last name?" Suddenly, he remembered that conference he went to that included training with stressed and/or distressed beings. Then he had an idea of how to proceed. "I am interested in your offer to set me free. What I would like from you now is more information." *Nailed it, that's exactly what they told me to say in this type of situation. Make the subject feel at ease and in control while giving you relevant information. Who knew that stuff would ever come in handy*?

"You are the head of security, correct? What about your very pressing issues?" Scythe asked.

"Don't worry about that. You just tell me why you're here, and then I'll deal with those other matters."

Instead of answering, Scythe raised a hand in his direction, but he wasn't pointing. His fingers were too loose. Crash felt a searing pain in his right hand, his left leg, and his belly. Those were, coincidentally, all of the places where he had had surgery to fix various ailments with artificial parts.

"What are you doing?" Crash asked, through gritted teeth, his hand spasmed and the weapon fell to the ground with a clatter.

Scythe stood up and crossed the room frighteningly fast. He placed his hand on Crash's throat. Crippled with pain, Crash was unable to fight back.

Scythe bent down and whispered in his ear, "I said, I'm here to free you. And free you I shall. I will free all of you. And you will be so much better off. Before this is over you will be on your knees thanking me."

Crash was fighting to stay conscious, but he couldn't breathe. *Think.* He remembered the alarm button under his desk. He pushed it with his left hand. It was the last thing he remembered.

17

Lyra burst into the waiting area with Ian trailing behind and carrying his portable equipment. She looked around. Whatever she was expecting, this wasn't it. Everything seemed relatively normal and quiet.

"What's going on, Gorb?" She had long ago figured out that Gorb knew everything. How he knew everything, however, was still a mystery.

"Hi, Lyra!" Gorb floated over to her. "What's going on? My robot friend got tired and took a nap or something, see?" he whispered and pointed to the corner of the room. Lyra frowned, a little while ago, she had never seen the robot so active, and now, to the best of her recollection, she couldn't remember ever seeing it completely shut down. The last thing she needed right now was a bipolar robot.

"Gorb, what happened?" she asked. "Did you shut MACRO off?"

Gorb held a few tendrils in the air. "I never touched him. I'd never hurt the little guy and I have a dozen surly witnesses to that fact." He indicated the patients scattered around the waiting area looking down at their phones. "Who's your boyfriend?"

"Oh," said Lyra as she felt her face get hot. "Um, this is Ian." Her eyes flicked up to him and he wore a smile. That would have to do for now.

"Ian, Gorb. Gorb, Ian. Oh, and the robot has a name it's MACRO. What's up with Vax and Nancy?" She knew that she could just barge in there and get the scoop from them, but the scoop was always more entertaining coming from Gorb, and frankly, she was getting tired of these things sneaking up on her.

"Vax and Nancy are very confused," he said. "They don't know why the patient is so creepy or how he's even alive. The patient was singing so loud I could barely hear the song on my radio, but then he quieted down a little and I could. Then I turned the radio off because of the little robot. I said it was voodoo. But they didn't listen."

Lyra and Ian exchanged worried glances over the voodoo comment.

Gorb swayed back to his desk, switched his radio back on, sat back down in his chair. He started humming an odd tune coming from the radio. Lyra wasn't up on the latest top forty trends, but if that's what was passing as pop music nowadays, she wasn't impressed.

"Thanks, Gorb," she said, even though in this case, Gorb's knowledge didn't clear up anything. She and Ian continued down the hallway toward Vax and Nancy and the zombie voodoo patient.

"Oh yeah," Gorb said, "you forgot to ask about Arthur."

Lyra stopped so fast that Ian ran into the back of her. Gorb was right. And if Gorb didn't volunteer the information in the first place, then it must be juicy. She turned around to backtrack, went around Ian, and peeked her head around the corner.

"What was that about Arthur?" she asked.

"He's in O.R. number four."

"So?"

"He's operating on a squid."

The realization washed over her. *No way.* "Thanks, Gorb!" She ran to O.R. four and threw the door open. "Arthur?"

"Not now, Lyra," he said.

He looked and sounded okay. *Good for him*, she thought.

"I'll be out of your hair in a minute," Lyra continued. "One, great job. I always knew you had it in you. And two, before all of this," she had no idea what *this* was, but for Arthur it was progress, "did you figure out what the deal was with MACRO?"

"I didn't have time, because this patient came in. MACRO was really worked up, though, rolling in circles with the beeping and the flashing light. Feel free to help yourself. I left his manual on Gorb's desk."

"Did you say he was active when you left?"

"Yes. Very."

Lyra frowned. She didn't want to bug Arthur anymore and throw him off his game, but MACRO looked like he was shut down now. And if Gorb didn't do it, and Arthur didn't do it, then who did? She closed the door.

Ian was still there, trailing behind her with his scanning equipment. MACRO would just have to wait. She led Ian down the hall to where she had left Vax and Nancy. She didn't have to throw the door open though, because it was already cracked. That was unusual, too, and probably meant that they were as freaked out about the whole thing as she was. *Good.*

"Hi guys," she said, entering. "Vax and Nancy, this is Ian. Ian, Vax and Nancy."

Nancy waved.

"Why is he here?" Vax asked. "And what's that?" He pointed at the portable scanner in Ian's hand.

For his part, Ian had gone white as a sheet again and was looking at the patient, who was still sitting straight up and was vocalizing softly.

"Is that your hot date?" Nancy asked.

Lyra chose to ignore Nancy for now. "Ian is on the space

station doing some experiments. And it just so happened that the timing of when his experiments went all wonky coincided with when our patient here got even stranger."

Nancy and Vax stared at her.

"Look," she said, "I'm well aware that this is a long shot, but it's all I've got right now. Do either of you have anything better?"

"What are you proposing here?" Nancy asked. "Hey, wait, did you say he's a scientist? Because he looks really familiar."

Ian gave Lyra a quizzical look. Lyra was afraid of being made fun of because of dating a web star, so she lied a little. *So sue me.* She gave Ian a *please keep quiet* look and figured she would just have to explain it to him later.

Lyra ignored Nancy again and approached the patient carefully, doubting that Ian would continue to cooperate if he didn't see that it was safe. She got as close to the patient as she dared and studied him. Then she whispered, "All I want is to give Ian a chance to use his portable scanning equipment on the patient. His equipment is technically for communications detection, but it's the same equipment that seems to have been affected by all of the changes. It could give us another angle on what's going on here." She turned to Ian and then back to the patient.

"Is this close enough, Ian? Are you more comfortable if I use the equipment?"

He nodded at her and looked frozen in place.

"Okay," she whispered. "Hand it over and tell me what to do."

He handed her the small scanner. "Why does he have a sword?" Ian indicated Vax.

"It helps him think," Lyra answered. Then she shook her head, remembering that everybody is intimidated by Vax, with or without the sword. She really should have warned him. She would have, too, if tonight weren't so crazy.

"I'm sorry, Ian. I really should have warned you about Vax. And I know that he looks scary, and doubly so with the sword, but he's a good friend, a good person, and a good doctor. I trust him with my life, and you can too. The patient, on the other hand, I'm not too sure about. Right now, I'm actually very happy to have Vax here with the sword. Because if anything in the next few minutes goes south, we might just need it."

"You think you guys are going to have to kill the patient?" Ian asked, his voice trembling and at least an octave higher than usual.

"Steady on, Ian. What I'm saying is that I'm scared, and right now Vax is making me feel better. Now how do I work this thing?"

The patient twitched, but didn't move. He did, however, continue with his light humming. And he smelled. Being this close to him, she could smell the faint, but very distinct smell of decomp. A fresh round of terror washed over her. Was the patient right in front of her sitting up, eyes open, humming, and dead? Something else was bothering her now.

Even more than the decomp and even more than the proximity. It was the song. *Oh no*, the song that this guy was humming was the same one that was playing on Gorb's radio. A chill ran through her body right down to her toes. She decided not to tell anybody just yet. Especially since she had no idea what it meant.

"Take a half a step forward and aim the pointy end of the scanner at his head," Ian said. His voice was wavering. "And then there's a trigger on the side. Hold the trigger down until it beeps."

"Then what happens?" Nancy asked.

"Then the data gets sent to my phone."

Lyra swallowed hard, trying to keep the fear out of her own voice now. "Meaning as soon as this machine beeps I can back up just as far as I want?"

"Yup. As far as the equipment is concerned, once there is a beep, we'll have all the data at our fingertips," Ian answered.

Ok, Lyra. You can do this. She glanced down at the scanner in her hand for a moment and located the button and the trigger. She pushed the button and aimed in at the patient's head, hoping that he or it or whatever would continue ignoring her.

"Here goes," she said, and pulled the trigger. Wait for the beep, he had said. She waited for the beep. She counted to three before she realized she was counting, but not breathing. She forced herself to take a breath and then started counting again. *C'mon, where's that beep*?

"Almost there," Ian said, as if reading her mind.

With her hand on the trigger and nothing else to do, she kept her attention on the patient, hoping for no sudden moves. Her hopes were fully dashed when he turned his head to look straight at her again. His eyes were glowing a feral bright green and yet they were vacant at the same time. She stifled a scream. He seemed to look both at her and through her at the same time.

Lyra froze in place, her heart beating out of her chest. She dared not stop the process of gathering the data, but now she was actively fighting every fight or flight instinct. Her senses heightened. She could hear Vax getting a better grip on the sword. And yet, even if she could will her feet to run, she wasn't at all sure they'd obey. She braced for whatever was going to happen next.

Beep.

The sound broke her out of her trance. She stepped backward several steps, slowly. Then she let out a deep breath. The patient was still staring at her, though, and she knew those eyes would haunt her dreams. That was if she was ever able to get to sleep again. Finally, the patient turned his head back the way it was before, staring at the wall.

Lyra gave out a little nervous laugh, a quiet one though, and looked around. They all looked every bit as tense as she was. Nancy crossed the room to put an arm around her as she continued backing out of the room. Ian went with them into the hallway and Vax stayed inside with his sword to stand guard.

Once out in the hallway, Lyra bumped into something and started wildly, nearly falling over. It was just Gorb.

"What in stars name is wrong with you, Gorb? For heaven's sake, you scared ten years off of my life." The way tonight was going she wasn't at all sure that she had ten years left, but she sure hoped.

Gorb wasn't acting sorry. "Yes, yes," he said, "the patient's scary, I get it. But I need your help. This is important."

"What's the matter?"

"It's the robot. I think he's sad."

Lyra couldn't believe that Gorb thought that the potentially sad robot was more important than patient zero brainwaves in there. Then she thought about Arthur not getting a chance to decode the signals that he had obviously been trying to send.

"Hang on a minute. Sad robot?" she asked. "Do you mean that MACRO is awake now? And what makes you think that he's sad?"

"Instead of a fast beep, it's a slow beep. And the circles are slower too."

"Is Arthur out of surgery yet?"

"Almost."

Lyra looked around. Ian was busy tapping out instructions for the data on his cell phone, and Nancy peered in on the patient and Vax, but didn't go back in.

"Hey, Lyra?" Ian asked.

She turned to him.

"I'm looking at some of the data. And, well, I'll be honest with you, it doesn't look like anything I've ever seen before. If I had to guess, though, I'd say it was some sort of signal."

"What's a signal?"

"The singing."

That surprised Lyra. "You think that weird vocalizing he's doing is a signal? A signal for what?"

"*I* don't think it's a signal," he said, "the *data* seems to suggest that it's a signal. A weak one, though. And how the hell would I know what it's for?"

"Okay," she said to him. "Sorry." She frowned. "Let's put a pin in that theory for a minute and check on MACRO. And there's something else, Ian." She led them back to the registration desk.

MACRO was indeed slow-beeping for some reason and going in circles. Just like Gorb had said. He perked up when he saw her, though.

"Hi MACRO," she said. "I know you're trying to communicate with us. Sorry about the delay." She picked up the manual right where Arthur said it was. Before she looked at the manual though, there was something she had to know. She switched on the radio.

The sound could barely be heard so she turned it up. Lyra felt a jolt of adrenaline as she recognized the tune. Gorb hummed along.

Nancy gasped. "That's the same tune that the patient is singing."

Lyra was thinking the same thing.

Ian gaped at her. "Turn it up," he said.

Lyra switched the volume even higher and it was clear that it was not an actual song on the radio, but it was the patient's song being transmitted via the radio station.

Lyra exchanged worried glances with Ian and Nancy. She switched to another station and then another, but it was the same thing. The patient's singing had taken over all of the stations. "What was that you said about the patient broadcasting a signal?" Lyra asked Ian.

"Fascinating," Ian said. "I'm going to sit down for a few minutes and look at this data more carefully," he said, indicating the waiting room chairs. It looked to Lyra that he was approximately at the sit down or fall down stage of stress anyway, considering everything that was currently going on.

"Hey, Nancy," she said, finding a train of thought forward. "Why don't you go and check other radios and see if they're picking up the same thing. Let's see just how far this signal goes. Yes?"

Nancy nodded enthusiastically, obviously happy to get out of the vicinity of the patient for a little while. "What are you going to do?" Nancy asked.

Lyra picked up the robot manual that Arthur had left on the desk. "I'm going to try to figure out what's wrong with MACRO. I think he's trying to tell us something."

"Yeah," Gorb said, "now that everything is back to normal, you have to cheer up my little buddy."

Lyra knew that everything was crazy, but she hoped that if she could figure out what he was trying to tell her, then maybe she'd be closer to fixing it.

She flipped through the manual. "Stars, how old is this model, anyway?" There it is, page thirty-four, communication. She groaned. "There's a four-page communication diagram. This is going to take forever."

Gorb floated to a position just over her shoulder and looked for himself. "You're overthinking this, boss. This will be fun, like we're playing charades, yeah?"

Lyra realized he was right, it was as simple as looking up the behavior code and matching it with the corresponding letters. It was tedious, but it was doable.

"You're right, Gorb, let's do this. Okay. The pattern seems to start with a slow counter clockwise circle, two beeps, and then a flashing red light." She scanned the manual until she found the corresponding letter. "R." She looked at Gorb and shook her head. "This isn't charades, it's more like hangman."

Gorb floated quickly over to the white board, erased the entire schedule, and grabbed the dry erase marker. He wrote the letter "R".

Lyra wondered if this would even work. What if he was in a loop repeating the same pattern over and over. There was no way she was going to figure it out if her only clue was the letter R.

There was another beep, though, and MACRO started another pattern. Lyra exhaled with relief.

Beep, clockwise, flash, beep.

Lyra flipped through the pages.

"I'm ready, what is it?" Gorb asked.

"E."

He wrote it down.

Flash, beep, flash.

Lyra was getting better at this, and she had to admit she was having fun. "B."

Beep, beep, back, forward, flash.

"Tell me again why you couldn't just download into a newer model?" Lyra scowled at the little robot. "O."

Gorb wrote it down.

Beep, beep, back, forward, flash.

"Okay, that's another 'O'."

Flash, flash, beep, beep, spin.

"T."

Gorb dutifully wrote the letter down.

A dark, lurking suspicion began to bother Lyra as she looked up at the last letter that Gorb had written on the board.

"Keep going, boss," Gorb said. "We're almost there, I can feel it."

"He wants us to restart him, Gorb." She could have kicked herself for not figuring it out sooner, or at least starting with that.

Ian looked up from his phone. "Oh yeah, look at that. It says "reboot." Then he went back to his data.

Lyra flipped through the book to figure out how to power MACRO off and back on again. It turned out there was a button behind his antenna that you had to hold down for six seconds until it beeped and then you had to let it go and then press it for another three seconds until it turned green again. "Come here, you," she said to the little robot.

"You think this will work? Will we get our funny little robot back?" Gorb asked.

Lyra shrugged. "I think so, at least that's what the manual says."

MACRO stopped spinning in a circle and then approached her before turning around to present the button.

"Either way, I'm pretty sure we figured out what he was trying to tell us. Hey, wait, it says here that if we get him reset properly, then there's a quick communication mode."

She pressed the series of buttons and waited to see what would happen next. Gorb put the dry erase marker back and came to watch too. She could even see Ian peeking over his phone, along with a couple of patients who apparently weren't quite nosy enough to know that ten minutes ago was probably the opportune moment to run for their lives.

MACRO slumped forward slightly and ceased all movement, flashing, and beeping. Then, when the button turned green again he sprang back to life.

Then there was so much beeping and flashing and circling that Lyra had no idea what to do. She flipped from the emergency communication mode to the quick communication mode.

Gorb ran back to the white board. "It looks like you fixed him, Lyra. But I think he's still trying to tell us something!"

"I think you're right again, Gorb. Are you ready?"

Gorb was so excited that he appeared to be vibrating in mid-air. "I'm ready!"

She glanced up at MACRO and then down at the guide. They got into a rhythm. Lyra watched and listened to MACRO and then called out letters, barely having time to make sure that Gorb was keeping up with it all. "S, C, Y."

Macro stopped for a moment for the first time since he had come back on. Lyra watched him, fascinated. Then he continued.

"T, H, E."

Then MACRO stopped again and looked at her. He gave her

the friendly little beep that he always gives her in the doctor's lounge.

"Ok," she said, looking at the white board, "I think he's done. What have we got?" Now that she wasn't concentrating on MACRO, she could still make out the faint singing of patient zero. "Scythe. What is that? Is that a thing? Ian? Have you ever heard of that?"

"Actually, it sounds a little familiar, maybe," he said, tapping out a search onto his phone.

She waited for him to finish. She glanced down at MACRO, remembering that he chose that ancient body on purpose. *Running from something*, Grayson had said. *Spooked.* Now she could identify with him.

And she still didn't know what was going on. Which was bad because on a space station in the middle of nowhere on the edge of a black hole, there was nowhere to run. And even if she could, she doubted that she would. This place was her home, for better or for worse.

Gorb fell into a new rhythm, humming along with the patient song. She had to fight the urge to sing along herself. She shook her head.

"Got it," Ian said. "At least, I think." He glanced up from his computer, and the worried look on his face did not make her feel any better. She crossed the room and sat down next to him.

Gorb followed her and shimmied over to where Ian was. MACRO stayed put.

"What is it, Ian?"

"Well, I got a few hits on the Scythe search. A couple of them look good, and one of them looks very bad."

"Describe very bad," Lyra told him, planning to lose patience if she had to ask him again.

"Like I said, there are a few options. One is a type of tree in the Massey system, one is a store at a shopping mall in Vega, and the third is a group centered around an escaped intergalactic mad scientist who is rumored to have turned himself into an Artificially Intelligent Being."

Lyra opened and then shut her mouth. She simply wasn't sure how to respond to that kind of information. "Oh come on! Why can't it ever be the store inside the shopping mall?"

"What do you think it means?"

"Well," Lyra said, "I don't know. Supposedly, MACRO went into that archaic and almost completely useless body in order not to get hacked. Grayson said that he was hiding from a hive mind, borg-type of group that he escaped from. Maybe he's just telling us what it is he'd like to stay away from?"

She felt stupid saying it. She knew it wasn't true, and that now really wasn't the time for optimistic assessments of their situation. Whether the people around her liked it or not, though, right now she was happy to be digging into denial.

MACRO beeped three times, the universal robot symbol for *no*.

"Shut up, MACRO," she snapped.

He rolled backwards.

"I'm sorry," she said. "I don't know what it was that I expected, but it wasn't that-whatever you just said. So, this Scythe is a person? Or an AI? Or a criminal?"

Ian re-read the information. "It's really not very clear on any of those points. There's only general and speculative information since the group is very secretive and obviously the leader is on the run."

Lyra crossed her arms. "Perfect. What do you think this group has to do with us?"

"Hey," Ian answered, sensing her change in mood. "Maybe it has nothing to do with us. You're the one who pulled me into this whole thing. And besides, the only thing we know for sure right now is that one of your, um, odder patients happens to be singing. And also, a really large rat started a bar fight. Right? Is that all or did I miss something?"

"Good point." He was right, in theory. She wanted badly to believe that she was overreacting, but she just had a feeling that things were not right. "Okay, a weird, singing patient, a giant rat, and a weirded-out robot. Things could be worse, right?"

That's when the patient stopped singing.

18

A dread washed over Lyra. If anything, the silence was even worse than the singing. She jumped up and ran to the radio and turned it up. Maybe it just wasn't as loud. She turned it up more, and then all the way. Nothing. She knew what it meant, and she didn't like it at all. It meant she had to check on Vax.

Vax made her think of Nancy. There was still no sign of her. Lyra glanced around the room to see if anybody else was going to volunteer before steeling herself to go back into the haunted room.

"Ok, people, so the weird singing patient is no longer singing. Maybe the lack of brain function finally caught up to him. That would, in fact, be completely normal. And a very rational explanation as to why he stopped. Just in case, though, I'm going to check on Vax."

Except that her feet wouldn't move. "Gorb, you coming with me, buddy?"

Gorb shook his head.

"What about you, MACRO? Up for a walk?"

Beep, beep, beep.

"Ian?"

"Um," he replied, pointing at his phone. "Research. Very important."

"Fine," she said, as she made her way slowly down the hall like she was being made to walk the plank in a pirate horror movie. "I'll go alone."

She rounded the corner. The door was still ajar. She peeked in, realizing that she was no longer breathing. She considered starting to again, but then decided it was best if she continued to just hold her breath. Vax was still standing guard and the patient looked to be in the same exact position with the same exact expression on his face as before, which was blank. She exhaled.

"The robot's beeping again, Lyra."

She was so startled that she literally jumped in the air. He had wafted in behind her. "Stop sneaking up on me, what is wrong with you?"

"Well, the robot's beeping and handsome guy wants you for something." He grinned. "And I know what it is," he said it playfully.

"Now is not the time for this, Gorb." She turned back toward the room and whispered to Vax. "I'll be right back." Then she made her way back to the waiting room, where MACRO was in fact beeping.

"Did you need something, Ian?"

"I've been looking over the data and I have a theory. But I'm afraid I can't test it if the guy isn't singing."

"What are you talking about?"

Beep.

"Well, the type of signal that we're hearing, in theory, could actually be disrupted if you had a strong enough competing signal."

Beep. Boop. Boop.

"Oh, get a real robot body," Lyra snapped. "I don't have the manual with me right now." She ran her fingers through her hair and then turned back to Ian. "I'm afraid I'm not following."

"Well, I obviously can't stop him from singing, but I think I could override the signal that he was sending to the radio."

Nancy came through the door, breathing hard. She opened her mouth to speak and then decided to breathe instead. She held up a finger for them to wait.

"Did you go all the way to the other end of the space station?" Lyra asked.

Boop. Beep.

Nancy nodded. "Yes. And the weird patient singing is top forty everywhere I went. In fact, the rowdies in engineering are nearing the breaking point. They want the old stations back."

"Don't we all."

"Wait, why don't I hear anything?" Nancy asked.

"Because he stopped singing," Lyra answered.

"Why? Hey, MACRO!"

Beep. Boop. Boop. Beep.

"I don't know why the patient picked now to stop singing. With any luck, maybe he's done," Lyra said it, but she didn't believe it. There was an eeriness that permeated the whole room.

"Is Vax still in there?" Nancy asked.

"Yeah, I just checked on him, he's fine."

There was a sound on the radio and Lyra realized she had left the volume all the way up. It sounded like the patient was still broadcasting live, and that he was taking a very long, very deep breath. Then there was a beat of silence.

Then there was a loud, screaming, inhuman noise that Lyra had never experienced before in her life. If what the patient was doing before was singing softly, now he was screeching in a pitch that was liable to cause hearing and nerve damage.

Lyra made a mad dash to the radio and switched it off, but the noise barely got any better. *That can't be good*. She unplugged it and the sound was the same.

Everybody in the room covered their ears and fell to their knees. Lyra did too, but only for a second. Then she remembered something. *Vax.*

She ran down the hallway, screaming even though she couldn't hear it over the noise. She reached in and grabbed the giant doctor by the shirt. He still had the sword in his hand, but he appeared frozen in place.

The patient, despite the change in volume and pitch of the sound emanating from him, had not changed his position or facial expression.

She pulled with all of her frenzied, terrified strength and managed to tug Vax out into the hallway. Then she slammed the door behind them.

With the door shut, the sound was, unfortunately, only slightly muted. Lyra turned and stared at the door for a moment, worried the patient was going to get up and come after them. *Where did that thought even come from*?

The pain in her ears was replaced by a ringing so pervasive it made her doubt the idea that there was a time that it never existed. *That doesn't make sense*, she told herself, but her body didn't seem to be listening to her brain anymore. Her feelings were even getting disjointed. It was like this new sound was affecting more than just her hearing. She and Vax made their way back to the waiting room.

The patients had all bugged out finally, leaving just Lyra, Vax, Ian, Nancy, Gorb, and MACRO. Lyra was finding it hard to think, but she fought through it. "Ian, you think there might be a way to disrupt whatever this is?" She was screaming over the noise.

He nodded. "I think so. It's all hypothetical though. The equipment I need is back in my room."

"Go get it, okay? I'll wait for you here."

"What are you going to do?" Ian and Vax shouted at her at the same time.

Lyra took a deep breath of resignation. "I think it's time to get Grayson down here."

Both Vax and Nancy's eyes got wide. Lyra turned from them for a moment to see Ian run out of the waiting area and wondered if he was ever going to come back.

Then she turned her expression back to Vax and Nancy. And Gorb, who had gathered with them at the thought of juicy gossip.

"No," Vax said. "You can't mean it."

"I do," Lyra said. "It's time for him to get his old butt down here."

She went to Gorb's desk where she knew there was a special phone that went straight to his cell phone. She picked it up.

"You think he'll be able to hear you?" Nancy asked.

"Oh, he'll hear me alright." She had to jam the phone to one ear while covering the other in order to hear the dial tone and then the ringing. It rang once, and twice and again. Nothing. His voicemail picked up.

"Hey!" she shouted. "In case you're still oblivious, we've got a situation in the waiting room that needs your attention. Got it? If you're not here in five minutes I will personally search this entire space station, find you, and drag you back here. Do you hear me? We need your help NOW! Oh yeah, this is Lyra." She hung up.

"I left a message," she shouted.

"We heard," they shouted back.

"Do you think he'll come?" Vax asked.

Nancy frowned. "I don't think there's any question he'll come. I think the only question is whether he's going to kill you when he gets here."

"At this point, it's either him or zombie patient guy, so I figure I don't have anything to lose, do I? Close your mouth, Gorb."

Gorb was, in fact, gaping, which was a very strange sight.

Lyra couldn't take it anymore and threw herself in a chair and buried her head in her hands. That's when the noise went to approximately half volume. She looked up at the others and found it slightly easier to think now.

Her phone rang. She jumped. Was it Grayson calling her back? It was Ian.

"I got here before the signal strength went down. Is it quieter there now?"

"Yes, it's quieter here, but we can still hear it."

"Okay, listen. I'm not one hundred percent sure yet, but I think that the signal is some kind of distress call."

"What?" Lyra asked. "We're the ones that are in distress."

"I know, right? But what I'm saying is that I don't think the signal itself is what we should be worried about."

Lyra felt her shoulders droop. "Oh no."

"Yeah, according to all of the data that my instruments are collecting, it's not the signal itself, but what that creature is calling to. And you should see my ratings! I just did a quick five-minute video blog about what's going on here and it's gone viral. Isn't that great?"

It's great if we're not all about to get killed, Lyra thought. "You think he's calling that weird AI evil scientist person?" She tried to whisper, but everybody in the room was in the process of scooting closer to her.

"Like I said, I'm just telling you what the data is showing. Pretty sure about the distress call, no idea of the end goal. No wait, in fact, distress call might even be the wrong term for it. A more specific explanation would be a homing beacon."

"That's not any better, Ian."

"I didn't say it was any better. Sorry, that's all I've got right now."

Grayson came bursting into the room. His hair was mussed, his coat was askew, and his face was red as a boiled lobster that had been drinking whiskey.

"Hey, Ian," she said, "I gotta go."

Grayson stopped in the middle of the waiting room and

glanced around. "What in the middle of holy hell is going on here, Lyra? And let me be clear that whatever it is, I'm holding you personally responsible because you're the one who called me in the middle of the night."

Lyra looked down at her watch. "It's nine forty-five."

"I can't believe I'm having to repeat myself here," he said and scowled at Vax and Nancy, who both took a few steps back. "What is going on here?"

Lyra stood her ground. "Well, you can hear the noise, right?"

Grayson frowned somehow with his entire face, not just his mouth. It was a terrifying sight. "The noise that sounds like fingernails on the chalkboard of my soul? Yes, I think I hear it. What is it?"

"It's the patient in room 22b." At least she hoped he was still there, she hadn't checked in a few minutes, but she was pretty sure.

Grayson rubbed his face with his hand. "Why, pray tell, is he making that noise, and why don't you shut him up?"

"We tried sedating him, sir. It didn't take."

"Well, why don't you up his dose?"

"We did. In fact, we upped his dose to about three hundred."

"Three hundred?" For the first time, Grayson looked like he was starting to wake up. "Then he wouldn't be singing, he would be dead."

"Well, about that," Lyra said and then remembered Vax had a copy of his chart. She crossed to Vax and held out her hand and he gave it to her.

She waved it at Grayson. "Look, he came in here nearly brain dead and he crashed after that. And then, well, he sort of just kept going on a downward slope."

He grabbed the chart out of her hand. "What are you talking about? Minus three hundred and eighty? That's not possible, Lyra."

"I know."

"DEAD people have a better brain function that negative three eighty."

"I'm aware. But Grayson, there's more."

"Should I sit down for this?" He didn't bother waiting for an answer and plopped himself down in the nearest chair.

"Ian says that-"

"Who's Ian? Does he work here at the hospital?"

"No, he's a visiting scientist."

"Bored," Grayson blurted out. "If this is a ghost story, then it's got a very bad beginning."

"Oh, I'm just getting started. As I was saying, Ian analyzed the patient."

"With what? Spreadsheets?"

"Can I just get through this?" Lyra asked. "I'm not sure we have that much time. This patient has a history of being unpredictable."

"You're telling me that double dead in there is unpredictable?"

"You're right," Lyra said, "I'm going about this the wrong way. Come on." She grabbed his hand, pulled him up, and led him to the room with the door that was now closed. "You should see for yourself. Vax, could you bring your sword?"

"I hardly think that's necessary." Grayson objected which was weird, he was fully aware that Vax never went anywhere without it. Maybe he was getting scared after all.

Lyra went down the hall and cracked the door open. The patient was indeed still sitting there singing. When the door opened, though, he swung his head in their direction.

Grayson screamed like a little girl. Lyra let out a scream as well. The patient's eyes were twice the size they should be and were now dripping a yellowish liquid. Lyra shut the door and backed away slowly. She watched the door carefully for signs of movement. Thankfully, there were none.

"So what do you think?" she asked Grayson.

He backed all the way out to the waiting room before he

spoke again. Then he frowned at her. "What you're telling me is that you can't handle even one weird, oozing patient on your own? You had to call me over here for this?"

Lyra could see the fear in his eyes, though. "Look," she said. *Stubborn old man.* "As I was saying, Ian analyzed the sound data and concluded that this patient is acting as some kind of signal."

She walked back over to Gorb's desk and turned the radio back on. Then she switched the station repeatedly, revealing the same awful sound.

"Lyra, what exactly are you trying to tell me here?"

"Ian thinks he's acting as some kind of homing beacon."

"You think that thing in there is calling something?"

"Yes."

"So what's coming?"

"That's the million-galactic-credit-question, isn't it? MACRO has been acting crazy lately, and when I reset him, he gave us a message."

"What was the message?" Grayson asked. This was as engaged as he had been since he had entered the room.

"The message was Scythe. Does that mean anything to you?"

"Oh no," Grayson said.

"What?" Everybody blurted out at him at once. "What does it mean?"

"Yeah," Grayson answered. "It means we're screwed."

"What are we in for, here?"

"I only know the name by reputation, in passing. But it's not good."

Emily burst into the room, looked around. Froze. Then looked like she was in the process of deciding whether or not to just bolt back out.

"Oh yeah," Gorb said cheerfully. "Emily was looking for you, Lyra."

"Emily!" Lyra said. She grabbed her arm before she could

wisely run off. "Welcome to the party. What is it that you needed to tell me?"

"And please tell me it had nothing to do with the rat," Grayson said.

"It is about the rat," Emily said. "Specifically, the guy that the rat bit."

"What?" Lyra asked.

"At the Frenzy incident. This guy got bit, but didn't tell anybody. Maura tracked him down. Genius here, just let a possibly infected patient just walk right out of there."

"I didn't see anybody get bit by a rat," Grayson said defiantly.

"Where were you, exactly, when the incident happened?" Lyra asked him.

"Behind the bar. I came out when it was over. Nobody said anything about an animal bite. He must have just slipped out unnoticed despite a dozen emergency medical personnel present. That's not on me, that's on him."

"What is it that you wanted to tell me about all of this?" Lyra asked.

"Oh yeah," Emily said. "I also did the necropsy on the Frenzy rat and there was a brain scan abnormality."

That made them all turn their heads.

"Why would you do a brain scan on a dead rat?"

"There were brain abnormalities, I did a scan out of curiosity, so sue me," she said and shrugged. "That's not the weird part, though."

Lyra was getting tired of hearing that.

"The weird part was that I was here when Maura's patient came in, the orc who got bit by the rat. He was exhibiting some very strange behavior. I was afraid it was a new drug version that we should catalog and did a brain scan on him too."

"And they both exhibited the exact same characteristics," Grayson finished her thought.

"Yeah, how'd you know? Despite the orc patient being nearly unresponsive, his brain activity was off the charts."

"Oh, this is bad," Grayson said.

"How so?" Lyra asked.

"I didn't want to tell you this unless I was sure. But this Scythe character, before he turned rogue, did most of his research on rats."

"What do you know about him?" Lyra and Emily both blurted out at the same time.

"Just urban space legend stuff, or so I thought," Grayson said. "Nothing that would be at all helpful in this type of situation."

"Well, if you're so worried about it, why don't you do something?" Lyra asked.

"Like what?" Grayson asked, wrinkling up his face. "What are you implying? Oh no you don't."

"Callista."

"Don't even say her name," he said, looking around nervously.

"But you said we were screwed."

"And we probably are."

Lyra could feel her blood pressure rising. "So why don't we get her?"

"Get her? No, I'm not going to get her, but that's not to say the situation probably doesn't warrant it."

Lyra balked. "So what, then, we should get Crash?"

They all had a good laugh at that.

"I guess he's our only option," Grayson said. "There's only one thing."

"What's that?" Lyra asked, wiping a tear away from her eye. It wasn't really that funny, but once the tension burst, even for a second, it was overwhelming.

"He should have been here by now."

Lyra's heart raced. He was right.

At that moment, red alert lights began flashing everywhere. Lyra swallowed hard. Only one guy could activate the station-wide alert and that was Crash. That meant that he was already involved, and it meant that really bad things were happening in more places than just the hospital. If he was in trouble, that didn't bode well for the rest of them.

"Look, we could use Crash's help, if he's not up to his eyeballs in danger already, but this is way above his pay grade, Grayson, and you know it. We need to tell Callista. We're out of options."

He shook his head. "No way." He looked very childish to Lyra, stomping his foot and refusing the only avenue of help available to them with the red emergency lights flashing around him like he was in the middle of some sort of dangerous disco.

She scowled at him and looking around to see if anybody else was going to jump in and help. They weren't. As usual. "You'd really rather face down an evil mad scientist invasion, or whatever the hell this is than go get the head administrator of the space station?" Lyra boggled.

"She's very scary."

How do you even know she's scary if you have never seen her? Yes, we've all heard the stories, but we don't even know for sure if any of them are true. We need her, Grayson, now."

He stood there and shook his head at her again. "You know how I got this job? After the last guy tried to go in there and summon her. They never found his body, you know."

"Summon her? She's not a genie, she's an administrator. She has office hours, for stars sake!"

"Then you go."

"You are the Chief of Medicine! You're in charge! And you're sending me because you're afraid?"

"You're adorable and people like you. I have no chance at all."

Lyra screamed in frustration. "Fine," she said at last. "I'll go get Callista. And you people should scan the zombie patient and see if his activity matches the orc bite victim and the Frenzy rat."

"If it does, then what does that mean?" Emily asked.

"I don't have any idea," she answered on her way out the door.

19

Callista's eyes flickered open. There was a beeping sound in her head. An alarm? She really shouldn't be surprised. After all, this is how she was always awakened. She looked around her office, sitting forward in her chair.

It happened in her chair this time. With her door closed. And by the looks of things, it had been quite a while. How long?

The clock on her desk still worked, the lit numerals telling her it was 11:04 a.m. but that was little help. The time of day didn't matter at all, not to her.

The wall calendar said 9283. A flicker of memory told her that wasn't up to date even before she fell asleep. She tried to move and failed.

Vulnerable. There was always that period upon waking that she was vulnerable to attack. Everything was quiet, though, so she sat for a moment and thought. She shut her eyes, hoping that when she reopened them again, she would still be conscious and she was. *It was true. Finally, she was awake again.*

Her computer. Yes. She turned it on. It immediately began trying to implement thousands of upgrades. She groaned. There was nothing to do but wait. Ten minutes later, according to the glowing clock on her desk, the computer gave up on the updates altogether saying that it wasn't compatible with current computer operating systems.

Yes, she thought, *that sounds about right*. Unable to figure out what the date was and still feeling vulnerable, she opened her top desk drawer. Weapons. Now these she remembered. She chuckled, grabbed her favorite mini pistol blaster, and placed it on top of the desk. Then she sat back and relaxed.

"Stupid Grayson," Lyra muttered the phrase in a mantra all the way to Callista's office. She had to look up the office location on her computer and double checked that she was arriving squarely within her posted office hours, which frankly, were pretty late for a Head of Space Station.

Then she continued all the way down the station's corridors, stopping only for a friendly wave to some of the people she knew as she was making her way there.

"The emergency lights really livened up the day," one friend said. "It's been a while."

"Does this have anything to do with you guys?" another one asked.

"Sort of," Lyra answered and continued on. "Stupid Grayson."

The other person nodded, as if it was an acceptable saying, and went along his merry way. It wasn't as crowded as it usually was in the travel arteries of the station, but that didn't mean that most people weren't going along with their own business. She had to give it to them, the people living here were a brave and steadfast bunch. And she was one of them, even if Grayson wasn't.

She began plotting her revenge on him in her head when she turned the last corner and realized she was in a part of the space station she had never been before. In fact, until she looked up the directions to this office she didn't even know this part of the station was here.

She continued along the eerie corridor, which would have been creepy even without the red flashing lights. She wished somebody would turn them off. They lost their adrenaline pounding allure within the first five minutes, and now they were just distracting her from her thoughts. And she needed all of her thoughts right now. There it was. Callista's office.

Lyra got to the door and stopped. She listened. There was nothing but a very eerie silence coming from the other side. How was it that all of this was going on, with the emergency lights and everything and Callista was just in there on her computer or whatever. You'd think she'd come out and have a look around. Although only a handful of people on the station claimed to have ever seen her and most of them weren't credible.

The door had what looked like a dragon logo carved into the wood, but now that she was staring at it very hard trying to get up the courage to knock, she could clearly see that the carving had several layers to it underneath. She nearly got mesmerized by the pattern.

Get it together, Lyra. It's just a door. We're all about to die. Maybe. Here, at the door, she understood Grayson's reluctance to come himself. She was here to tell the mysterious Callista about the life and death situation of unknown origin that they guessed was coming based on the prediction of a visiting neo-web star, the necropsy of a mutant rat, and the beeping of a mysterious, obsolete robot who had just started seriously communicating with them a few hours ago. And also, a medical mystery that may or may not be singing a message of their doom.

Her fist poised over the wood door and then hesitated for a moment. Her inner fear and uncertainty was doing battle with all of the space station alarms and flashing lights. She swallowed hard, took a deep breath, and then knocked.

Under normal, quiet, daytime working hours it would probably have barely been heard. Under current circumstances it was completely impossible. She tried to figure out what to do next. The obvious choice being to knock harder or to actually try the door handle, both of which she was afraid to do.

"Come."

The voice on the other side of the door startled her. She lost her nerve and her mind had to do battle with her body, which was screaming at her legs to run away. Callista was in there, alright. After crossing herself, Lyra turned the handle and eased the door open just enough to peek in.

A volley of laser blasts nearly greeted her face. She backed up around the wall again. The door, where the blasts had hit, didn't have a mark or a singe on it. Weird. After a few seconds, the volley of fire stopped.

Lyra, confused by the attack, said the only thing that came to her mind. "Callista? You can't shoot at me, these are your posted office hours!"

There was a long pause. "Who are you?" the voice asked.

"Oh yeah, I'm Lyra. And at the risk of pissing you off again, why would you tell me to come in and then shoot at me?"

Another pause. "I mean who are you? Are you my second in command?"

As far as Lyra knew there was no such thing as a Head of Space Station Second in Command. But she was pretty sure that if she had been so designated she'd remember. "Um, no. I'm just a doctor at the hospital here."

"Then go away, Dr. Lyra."

"Oh, hey, it's just Lyra to you. We're on the same team here, right? Look, you are in charge of this entire Space Station, right? And we are under attack, sort of. As you can see from all of the flashing red lights and alarms and stuff." For the first time, she was actually grateful to all of the annoying lights for adding a certain gravity to her words. "Have you, um, noticed any of that at all?"

"Yes? Why are you here?"

"I told you. Alarms. Emergency. Attack. Something's about to go down, I'm telling you. And we need your help."

"What are the rumors?"

"What?" Lyra was unable to keep the fear and the frustration from coming out in her tone, but Callista seemed to be out of it somehow, and hopefully wouldn't pick up on it.

"About me? What are the rumors," Callista asked.

"Do you really think now is the time?"

There was more shooting.

"Fine, alright, stop! Some people swear you are a shifter. Or part vampire. Part goddess. Flesh over evil robot. I mean, I could keep going, but what's the point? Are you going to help us or not? You think there's any chance I'd be here if we weren't really, really desperate?"

Her plea was met with more laser fire and another, "Go away."

"Screw this," said Lyra. "Thanks for nothing!" she called out as she ran back down the hallway to the normal part of the station.

Once she was a sufficient distance away, she slumped against the wall and closed her eyes to think, which she had to do because of the still flashing lights.

And then it hit her, there was a trio of problems on the station right now that she knew of. She'd decoded MACRO's messages and Ian figured out the patient was sending a signal. There was still one more piece of the puzzle, and she knew just who to go to in order to figure it out. *Maura.*

20

Maura smiled when Lyra entered the room. "Girl, it's been too long." She offered coffee, bravely ignoring the emergency lights.

Lyra shook her head and sat down.

"You're here about all of this, aren't you?" She gestured with her hands toward the seizure inducing lights all around. "Are we all gonna die or what?"

"I don't know about you, but I'd like to avoid that."

"How can I help?"

"Rats. Tell me everything you can about these rats."

Maura raised an eyebrow. "The rats are unusual. What am I saying? They're nuts. They're exhibiting completely abnormal behavior and feature an enlarged size. But other than the one that started the bar fight, they haven't shown any aggressive behavior. In fact-" Maura's voice trailed off.

"What?" Lyra asked, taking a seat across from Maura.

"It's crazy," Maura said.

"Trust me, with what's already happened today I'm desensitized to crazy."

"Well, I can't be sure, but it feels to me like they're *waiting* for something. How weird is that?"

Lyra thought it over. If Ian was right, and the patient was calling something evil to them, maybe they were waiting for whatever it was calling. If whatever they were facing was planning on using a rat army, this was bad. Her blood ran cold.

"As much as I hate to say it, it sort of makes sense to me."

Maura raised an eyebrow.

Lyra decided to tell her, if there was going to be the slightest possibility of a rat army in her immediate future, then she wanted Maura on her side. The problem was, the story she had to tell felt more outlandish every single time she tried to tell it. She took a deep breath. "So, um, there might or might not be a weird zombie patient emitting a signal that could be a sort of homing beacon to draw an evil scientist called Scythe here."

Maura's expression changed to reflect the fact that she believed Lyra was screwing with her. But Lyra made very clear she was not. That caused Maura to open her mouth to argue and then shut it again.

Maura looked thoughtful and tapped on the desk. "We're friends," she began, "and I'm going to go ahead and try to roll with this. But the big question in my mind is, why would you think any of that?"

"Well, you know the famous web scientist Ian?" *People were going to figure it out eventually anyway,* she thought.

She nodded. "A little."

"Well, this patient had us stumped, so I got the idea to bring him in and use this data analyzer on him to see what was going on."

"That doesn't sound like medical protocol."

"Desperate times." Lyra shrugged.

"This was your idea? How do you know Ian?" She smirked.

"He's visiting Celestica, and yes we've been dating."

"Tell me everything," Maura said, leaning forward. Her eyes lit up.

"Nothing to tell, I mean it's going ok as far as I'm concerned." The emergency lights that continued to flash reminded Lyra that she didn't have a lot of extra time to chat, especially since Callista wasn't going to help them.

"Figures. So you had a hot date and then some data analysis?" She looked dubious.

"Oh, there's also MACRO, he's freaking out."

"Is he the robot that hangs out in the doctor's lounge?"

"Yeah, how did you know?"

"Oh, he's the focus of all kinds of gossip."

"Really? Short robot, communicates with beeps and flashes? Blue fin on his head?"

"Yep, that's him," Maura answered.

Now Lyra had a lot more questions, but they'd have to wait. "MACRO freaked out. He was trying to tell us something, and when we started deciphering his message, it spelled out Scythe. Apparently, that's an evil, escaped scientist that may or may not have turned himself into an AI."

"You think this AI person is going to come here and use his rat army to attack us?"

Finally, Lyra thought, *somebody gets it*. "Well, I don't know, but if the events are all connected, and I hope they're not, then we're obviously going to need your help."

Maura smiled and started digging through her paperwork and then her face fell. "I'm going to be very limited in what I can do, the regulations for pest control of rat species are very specific and..."

Lyra stood and shook her head. "No regulations, no rules. If I send you a message, then it's going down. Bring all the firepower you can to the ER waiting room. And by the way, I think that the AI component negates all of the natural-species regulations, does it not?"

"Oh yeah." Maura's face brightened. "No rules?"

"No rules. If I call you, I want maximum carnage. Everything you've got. Nothing less than total extermination. Got it?"

"Okay," Maura answered. "Total extermination. I love it. Just give me a few minutes to get everything together."

~

Once Lyra got back out into the hallway, she called Ian on her cell phone. "Hey, how are things over there?"

"Well," he said, "I got the communication disrupter equipment back to the emergency waiting room, but not much has changed. The emergency lights are still going off and we're just waiting. Oh, your little robot is flipping out again."

Uh-oh, Lyra thought. There was a commotion sound on the phone for a moment.

"This is Grayson. Lyra? What's going on? Can you see about getting these idiotic lights and sirens turned off? If this whole thing goes south, is it too much to ask to be obliterated in peace and quiet? And who knows, without all of this racket I might actually be able to come up with an idea."

"Oh, you are a piece of work," Lyra said.

"What?" he asked.

"You're asking me to check on Crash."

"Well, you are on the other side of the station, correct," Grayson asked. "Technically you're closer."

"I hate you. And give Ian his phone back." She hung up before he could think of any more suicide missions to send her on.

She stopped to try and think. Grayson certainly had a point with the alarm system becoming a bother. But what about Crash? If something bad happened, she could be walking into a trap. But then again, she had already dealt with a mutant rat, Grayson, a freaked-out robot, a zombie patient, and whatever the hell Callista was. Because she didn't clear that up any. What was one more mysterious disaster?

She looked down at herself. Nothing but a white coat with

pens and forms and sticky notes in her pockets. She had nothing on her that would help with any kind of self-defense. What she wouldn't give for a weapon. What an odd thought. Believe it or not, she had never really felt unsafe before here on Celestica.

Carl! Everybody on Celestica knew the super cool werewolf doorman that worked at the Frenzy. If anybody could help her, he could. She took off at a run. Thankfully, it wasn't too far.

With the emergency lights flashing, of course it was packed. She fought her way through the crowd outside the door toward the friendly doorman.

He caught sight of her and motioned her forward with his hand. She continued to fight her way to the front, hearing a chorus of grumbles as she skipped everyone.

She finally reached Carl, who looked down at her quizzically. "You do not look like you're trying to get in. Too serious. And in work clothes. Or are you into that?" He grinned at her and winked.

She got really close to him, so she could try some semblance of a whisper. "Look, I've got to do something dangerous." She pointed above her to the flashing lights. "Top secret. And, um, I need some protection, if you know what I mean." He produced an entire packet of condoms from somewhere in his pocket. "Girl, I feel ya, here ya go."

Lyra shook her head.

"Um, not that kind of protection. The rowdies kind of protection. Unless you have a weapon on you right now that you'd let me borrow?"

"I do not, milady, but I guarantee you that almost everybody in there does," he pointed toward the inside of the crowded bar. "Especially tonight. Make your way to the back left of the room, follow the drunken shouting, and ask for Merck."

Lyra leaned over and kissed him on the cheek. "If we all survive this, I'm going to owe you one."

"You and half this space station, baby."

Lyra made her way inside and weaved through the drunken, loud revelers. The place had the for-once appropriate feel of an end of the world party. She made her way toward the area Carl spoke of. Then she started shouting over everybody to find Merck.

Just when she began to get frustrated trying to get around in the boisterous crowd, there was a tap on her shoulder.

"How bout the end of the world, baby? You need a little loving from the Merck?" A tall, lean, orc loomed over her, the horns on his head were gleaming in the dark. He wore jeans, a white t-shirt and a purple bandanna.

"Are you Merck?"

"Who wants to know?" He smirked, not realizing he had already let the cat out of the bag. She wondered how much he had been drinking.

"Look, I don't have a lot of time to convince you or negotiate or anything, but I need a weapon. You see, I'm trying to save the Space Station. I promise I'll bring it back. I mean, minus a bunch of bullets probably. But, if we survive, I'll pay you back. I'm totally good for it." She raised her hand in a goofy scouts-honor signal.

He stared at her without blinking, obviously trying to figure out what in the hell to say to the weirdest proposition ever. Maybe. Lyra certainly didn't know his life.

"Why you?" he asked after a long pause.

"That's a damn good question. Why always me? I mean-"

"What I'm asking," he cut in, "is where are all the other people trying to save the station? I mean, here I am drinking the blue devil here waiting for security to fix everything. Because they usually do. Are you telling me that the fate of the space station is in the hands of a cute doctor soliciting illegal weapons from a nightclub?"

He had a point. How do these people keep roping me into doing everything for them? Oh yeah, they won't do it themselves. "Oh sure, when you put it like that it sounds bad," she said. "Hey, look, are you saying if I was a large guy with a sword, you'd just hand me a gun and believe him?"

"No, I totally believe you. Something about the panicked look in your eye." He got closer. "Oh yeah, I've seen that look before. You've seen action, haven't you?" He smiled. "Well, you've got more than you bargained for, tonight. That's for sure. I'll loan you a gun, a really good one. I have several on me right now."

Where? she thought. Lyra searched his jeans with her eyes for weapons before realizing that it looked like she was ogling him and brought her eyes back up to his face. "Can I see it?"

"Excuse me?" he said with a smirk.

"Look," she got really close to his face, and judging by the looks on his companion's faces, they expected her to kiss him, "in your dreams, but that security you talked about, who's in charge of them?"

"That idiot Crash."

"Yeah, that's right. And who has the only controls to the system wide alarms?"

"Crash?"

"Yeah, and who do you think I'm going to check on right now?"

Some of the blood drained from Merck's face, and his expression finally flickered with awareness and something else, maybe even genuine alarm.

He swallowed. "Okay, I'm in." True to his word, he produced a gun from his back pocket and handed it to her. "Okay, doctor lady, let's do this."

"I'm so sorry, I forgot to introduce myself," she said. "I'm Lyra. And you don't have to come. I only asked for the weapon."

"I know. That's why I said you got more than you bargained for." He grinned and turned toward the exit, weaving through the crowd much faster and more effectively than she had coming in.

21

Merck and Lyra came to a stop outside Crash's office. The doorway was left wide open. Lyra wasn't sure whether that was a good sign or not, she had never checked on him in his office before. She held up a hand to hold Merck back for a second while she peeked inside.

She didn't see anything. She frowned. What she expected was carnage. Blood on the walls, something like that. But it looked like nobody was home. "It looks okay," she told Merck and motioned him inside with her.

The first thing she did was to start looking around the room for a button or something. "Hey, Merck, I've heard that there's a button in this room can turn off all of the emergency lights."

"But isn't this an actual emergency?" he asked.

"Yes, but as it turns out all these idiotic lights do, after the first few minutes, is keep us from being able to think. Especially in the hospital. Trust me, once the lights are off, we're still going to save Celestica."

She spotted a hand on the floor. Crash was laying under his desk.

Oh no. She ran to him and knelt down to take his pulse.

"Merck, keep an eye out." The pulse was weak, but there. She rolled him over and started CPR.

"Come on, Crash. You're too idiotic to die like this." She got Merck's attention and tossed her phone at him. "Call Nancy. Tell her I need a team here right away for Crash at his office. Unknown injuries, thready pulse, not breathing."

Merck dialed Nancy. "Hello. Um, I'm Merck, you see and-"

"Hurry!" Lyra said.

"Um, Crash is hurt and not breathing and-"

"Nancy!" she yelled it loud enough so that Nancy could hear. "Put us on speaker."

Duh, why didn't I think of that in the first place?

"Lyra?"

"Nancy, Crash is injured. Looks like a choking injury. I need a team here now."

There was silence on the other end for a moment. Then she heard Nancy's voice in a stilted tone. "Um, hello, this is Nancy at the Emergency Room. I'm afraid we are very busy at the moment and we are not going to be able to send a team at this time."

"Nancy? What the-" Click.

"Did she hang up on you?" Merck asked, raising an eyebrow.

"It appears so." Lyra frowned. "Something must be wrong."

Merck put Lyra's cell phone on the desk and made himself useful looking around for buttons while she continued helping Crash. "Um, Lyra? I think you should look at this."

"I'm a little busy at the moment." Lyra pounded on Crash's chest and worried. *What is going on at the waiting room? Should she go and help them? But she can't leave Crash like this.* She bent down to give him a breath and then looked up at Merck. "Hey, Merck, want to learn how to do CPR?"

"So you can go running around saving the space station and leave me kissing Crash? Hard pass. But look, on Crash's computer, there's a crazy figure on the screen. This must have been what he was looking at when he was attacked."

"Well, what does it look like?" Lyra asked.

"It looks like a guy in a mask and a hood."

"That doesn't help very much."

"Well, it's scary. If you could see it, I think you'd be a little more freaked out than you are. Hey, it's a video, hang on." He pushed some keys on the keyboard.

A minute or two passed while he watched the video and she did CPR.

"Oh, man," he said at last. "It looks like that guy killed Celestica's gatekeeper. Just left him there on the floor."

Lyra swallowed. "That's terrible." Things were deteriorating fast now. Merck started rummaging around the room again.

"Hey, look, I found some buttons."

Lyra looked up and the emergency lights stopped flashing. "Hey, great job." At least something was going right. She breathed into Crash again and then looked up while she pounded on his chest to continue trying to convince Merck to stay and take care of him.

Crash regained consciousness. He started coughing and looked up at her.

"Crash!" she said.

He just put his hand to his throat and rolled over. She put a hand on him to steady him. "Slow down there. What happened?"

He coughed and sputtered some more.

"Slow down, Crash." She looked up at Merck. "You think you could find him some water?"

Merck jumped into action. A minute later he had a little paper cup. The two of them helped Crash to a sitting position with the wall for support.

"Attacked," he sputtered.

"Who attacked you, Crash?" She watched him take a sip of water.

"Halloween costume guy." He took another sip of water.

"Did he have a name?" Lyra asked.

"He had a weird name. Said he was going to free us all. Then he started using the force or something. And then he started choking me."

Lyra took a deep breath and looked at Merck for a moment. "Hey, Crash, he didn't by any chance say that his name was Scythe, did he?"

"Oh yeah, that's the one," he gasped.

"Did he say anything else, Crash?"

Crash shook his head.

Lyra's phone started playing a dance song. Merck and Crash both looked toward the noise sound like it was insane.

Merck spoke first. "Is somebody's phone playing the hit song: If a booty shakes in the wilderness, can anybody hear it?"

Lyra jumped up and grabbed the phone.

Crash grinned weakly. "I love that song."

Lyra answered it. "Hello? Nancy? He's there, isn't he? What does he look like? Oh no. Ok."

Grayson must have grabbed the phone from Nancy, because his voice whispered to her next, "We need help, Lyra. I've got an armed to the teeth lawyer, what can you bring to the party?" Lyra thought. "Ok, Grayson. I'll see your lawyer and raise you a regulation-free pest control badass. See you soon." She hung up.

Merck and Crash looked at her. "It's an emergency ring tone, ok? Between me and Nancy. Tell anybody and I'll kill you both, but right now we have bigger problems. Crash, the person who did this to you is at the emergency room waiting area and he's causing problems. And it gets worse."

"How could it be worse?"

"He has some kind of rat army."

"Um, yeah. That is worse," Crash said, struggling to get to his feet.

"Where do you think you're going?" Lyra asked him.

"I'm not going to let you guys walk in there and fight him without me. I'm the only security-"

"You're the only security this space station needs. I know, so you keep saying. But you're hardly in any shape to fight."

"Maybe not, but I have no shortage of fun weapons. You guys look over there." He pointed outside the open door. Lyra peeked, though, and he punched in a code somewhere in a desk and it opened a hidden closet. The weapons inside were impressive.

Merck's face lit up. "Now we're talking!"

"But you can barely walk," Lyra protested as the guys loaded up on laser rifles.

"That's okay," Crash said, "my trigger finger works fine. Hey, didn't you mention a rat killer?"

"Oh yeah, Maura." Lyra smiled. Give me a second." She grabbed her phone.

~

Lyra, Maura, Merck, and Crash were a very strange, heavily armed group who earned barely a sideways glance as they made their way toward the emergency waiting area. They slowed as they approached the door.

Lyra figured that the only thing they had going for them now was the element of surprise. She held her breath and quietly turned the handle. The door opened without a sound. She continued to hold her breath.

"Finally!" A booming voice met her ears with a metallic twang. In fact, it took Lyra a few seconds to realize that the guy in the Halloween mask in the middle of the emergency waiting area, the one flanked by a bunch of large rats and holding everybody at bay, was talking to her.

"You, Lyra, get in here. It's about time."

So much for sneaking up on him and saving everybody, Lyra thought.

Scythe stood tall in the center of the room and seemed to be holding everybody back with a hand. *What is he, using some kind of psychic power?* That must have been how he overpowered Crash. The rats were pacing back and forth behind him, eyeing the crowd hungrily.

"You were waiting for me?" Lyra asked him. She leveled the small pistol that Merck had given her at him. "I really don't know what to say." She aimed and pulled the trigger.

"No, don't!" Grayson yelled.

Scythe wasn't intimidated, in fact, he didn't even seem to blink. He continued to hold eye contact through the mask. There seemed to be some kind of force field in place. The laser blast ricocheted off the invisible wall without affecting him. Everybody else jumped out of the way.

"You can't shoot him, Lyra. Why do you think we're all just standing here, because we're morons?" Grayson got up off of the floor and went back into position with his hands up.

"Well," Lyra began as she intended to answer Grayson. She didn't get to finish, though, because Scythe started to laugh at them. *Rude.*

"I told you," the guy twanged in his metallic accent, "I am Scythe and I came here to set you all free."

Lyra looked around at everyone to see if they knew what the guy was talking about. "I'm sorry, but what in the black hole are you talking about? And what is that thing on your face?"

The group around her let out a collective groan.

"Well, Sorr-ee," Lyra said. "But I honestly don't know."

"For eons," he said dramatically, stopping to take a deep breath and preparing to launch into a prepared monologue the others had probably already heard, "I have studied intelligence in the cosmos."

"I'm sorry," Lyra said, "I didn't catch your name."

He stopped, as if processing the statement. "You're asking me what my name is?"

"Yes, who in stars name are you and what are you doing on my space station?"

Everyone around Lyra nodded seriously.

He threw his head back and laughed. "It's funny, I reap creatures with intelligence and they serve me. But you, Lyra, with this witty, insubordinate streak. Well, I've missed that and I haven't encountered it in quite some time. I cannot wait to absorb you into my consciousness."

"No thanks. I asked what your name was," Lyra continued.

"Scythe. You may call me Scythe," Scythe answered Lyra's question, but his face was contorted in rage at being questioned. Or at least it appeared so through the mask, which bunched at the edges.

“What's with the mask, anyway?” Lyra knew she was getting to him, at least a little bit. She had no idea if irritating him was going to hurt or help. Judging by the combination of dirty looks she was getting, nobody else did, either. "Ok. Go on."

"I was going to," he said, narrowing his eyes. "And no matter what you currently think, Lyra, you will be bowing to me soon enough."

Doubt it, Lyra thought as loudly as she could. Maybe if she could get him to drop his guard for a second, they could rush him. *Oh no, she was thinking again. Was he able to read minds*?

What was this guy's end game here, anyway? To stand there and talk us to death or to take us on all at once? And if he could do that, then why did he need a force field and a rat army?

"As I was saying," Scythe said, "I'm here to free you all. For eons I have been studying intelligence in the cosmos. Mostly small, unattached, undeveloped intelligence. But then I grew horribly bored and decided it was time to move onto more complex organisms. Except like you, Lyra, they always resisted. They always plotted against me-"

"Wait a minute, Scythe. I have a question." She raised her hand as if she was in school. "Exactly why were you waiting specifically for me?" Lyra asked, cutting in.

Scythe stopped again. He took a deep breath and closed his

eyes for a moment. "Because I want the best, you see. The smartest. When I make my new slaves, I want among them the person in charge."

"I'm in charge, here!" Grayson boomed.

"Yeah, show's what you know," Lyra answered, pointing at Grayson, "he's in charge."

"Your pretend pecking order is meaningless to me. I can read all of your minds. Nobody here cares about what he has to say."

"Hey!" Grayson said.

"They have been here waiting for you, Lyra, to come and save them. In fact, from a cursory reading now that you've arrived, I see that this is it, the entire cavalry. You see, what I want is you, as my second in command, forever."

"Huh," thought Lyra, who had never heard that phrase, second in command, her whole life and yet had heard it twice already today. Both by weirdos. *Figures*. Nobody real was running around offering her promotions.

"You, Lyra, can save me from the infinite boredom of running my kingdom," Scythe continued, "of constantly having to tell idiots what to do. And you don't stand a chance against me, so let's begin."

“Wait,” Lyra said, although now she was just buying for time. “If you’re here for me, and you say you are. Then I deserve to see. I want to know what you look like. Under the stupid Halloween mask. Or are you scared?”

Lyra swallowed and Scythe froze. She was afraid that she had taken it too far this time. The room went completely silent with everybody wondering what in stars name was going to happen next.

Scythe’s black-gloved hand went toward his face. He grasped and then removed the mask. Everybody in the room who could see him gasped.

Scythe had only sunken holes for eyes, although he still seemed aware of everything going on in the room. The skin on his face was a sickly, oily green that was barely hanging on. Lyra tried and failed to stifle a scream and her heart started racing. What exactly were they dealing with here? And how was this guy still alive?

"Ian," Lyra said, not even trying to hide the newfound fear in her voice, "what about that disrupter?"

"Sorry, Lyra. It has the same effect as the laser blast. He has some kind of psychic force field or something.

“Lyra,” Scythe said, “you got what you wanted, a peek behind the mask. And now, I’m afraid your time is up.”

Think, Lyra. There was no time to think, however, as Scythe pulled out a small, oval orb with a ticking clock on it. In large, laser, projected numbers bigger than the object itself, a count-down clock was running. It was down to thirty seconds.

"Has that thing been on this whole time?" Lyra asked. The bomb, if that's what it was, would not only kill everybody in the room, it would seriously damage the space station. How was it possible for this thing to keep getting worse?

Scythe closed his eyes and pointed at the door, the only exit in the room except for the ambulance bay exit which was currently blocked by him and his force-field.

Fifteen seconds.

"No, no, no," Lyra screamed, "get to the door, quick." Merck got there first and pounded on it. It was too late. Somehow, Scythe had sealed it from the inside.

Ten seconds.

"Wait," Lyra screamed, "it's me you want, open the door and let them go."

"No, I want all of them, plus you," Scythe answered. "I told you that I'm going to free you all."

"So you keep saying," Lyra said. "But a bomb seems a very weird, and frankly unfriendly way to do it. And if you get a second, could you please put the mask back on?"

"You see, like the rats here, I've been experimenting with reanimating brain matter. Infusing it with my own power. But first, in order to do that, I have to-"

"Kill us." Lyra finally understood what was going on here.

"That's right." Scythe smiled at her.

She had to fight to not retch. "And then you'll turn us all into weird A.I. zombies?"

"If that's your preferred term, then sure."

"Like the patient you sent us, a mindless, soul-less homing beacon."

"Ah, Ben," Scythe said. "Great job, Ben, by the way," he shouted back toward the patient rooms.

This can't be happening, Lyra thought. *I can't die and then be ugly and undead like this.* She thought about the patient behind Scythe, and then the other patient rooms and then she remembered Arthur. *Arthur*! As far as she knew, he had never come out from working on the Cephalopod patient. Maybe he was still back there.

"Arthur!" Lyra yelled. "Arthur, help!"

The clock on the bomb ticked down, this time with a robotic auto-voice vocalizing the last five numbers in addition to the visual representation. "Four, three, two..."

Lyra felt a wave of sadness that these people had thought that maybe she could save them and yet she couldn't. She closed her eyes.

The metallic voice said "One, one, one, one..."

Lyra cracked an eye open. *MACRO*. He was able to sneak up behind Scythe because he was over at Gorb's desk. It looked like he was jamming the bomb's transmission somehow. Arthur came running around the corner behind Scythe screaming and brandishing a cutting saw.

The surprise in Scythe's face from the bomb not going off was priceless, and gross. And then he wheeled around to face Arthur.

This was it. This was their chance. Lyra felt her face contort into a snarl. "MACRO's blocking the bomb. Get him!" Lyra screamed, and then charged.

Arthur got to Scythe for a moment, but then was thrown against a wall on the opposite side of the room. That meant that Scythe's force-field was down. The other evidence of that was the rat army was loose now.

Vax came out swinging with his sword, doing his best to keep the rats at bay. Maura was also doing damage to the rats, taking them out with a blaster and a scream. Ian hit Scythe with the disrupter ray before he could put the force-field back up.

Crash and Merck created thunderous booms, aiming their weapons fire at the evil mad scientist in the center of the room. And every once in a while, Floyd got a shot in too.

"One, one, one..."

Lyra swerved away from Scythe so she wouldn't get caught in the crossfire and dove behind the desk where MACRO was. "Hey, MACRO. I could kiss you. Good job, little buddy. Keep up the good work, ok?"

"One, one, one..."

Lyra peeked up behind the desk and got an idea. She watched the orb bomb swaying perilously in the hands of the mad scientist. "Hey, MACRO? If I get that orb and bring it over here, do you think you could disable it?"

MACRO beeped yes.

"One, one, one..." the voice continued.

Taking a deep breath, Lyra screamed as she ran. "Hold your fire, people!" Scythe's face turned to her as she had purposely attracted the entire room's attention. It was clear that Scythe expected her to attack somehow, and so he was taken aback when Lyra instead swerved and grabbed the orb out of his hand and headed back to Gorb's desk.

"Ok!" she screamed. "You can get him again." She bent down and put the orb in front of the little robot. "Do your thing, MACRO. And thanks."

Vax was making headway against the rats, but despite being able to get the orb away, Scythe was winning the battle against everybody else. All of the weapons appeared to be useless against him, even without the force field.

She heard Arthur scream and looked up. The zombie patient from 22b was upright and attempting to fight him. The patient was doing it clumsily, and in a perverted looking way which made it all the more horrifying. She looked at the chaos and fighting going on in the room. *Now what?*

22

With that Lyra person long gone, Callista sat back, gun in hand, and bided her time. Soon her strength and power would return. Soon, she could go forth and figure out what exactly was going on.

Either this Lyra minion was telling the truth, and the station itself was in trouble, which would explain the alarm, or she was the threat herself, in which case she would be dead. Either way, it would be handled and soon. She tapped a finger absent mindedly on the distressed wooden desk.

All of her office furniture looked dated and covered in dust. Pity. It had all been recently renovated when she fell asleep, at least that was one of her last memories. When she closed her eyes, she tried to remember, to recall the former things, but as usual they came only in bits and pieces.

Then there was the alarm of course, the beeping going off inside of her head. She knew that wouldn't shut off, not until she'd neutralized the threat. She was able to tap her feet. This waking up was going faster than the last one. Either she was getting better at it, or the threat was more grave than she expected. Either way, as soon as she could physically get up, the beeping would transform into something real, a map inside her head leading her toward whatever threat needed to be neutralized. Such was her role, and the absence of said role had caused her to go to sleep. She hated going to sleep.

What if I simply don't save the space station? Will I stay awake then? Probably not. If the space station were to be destroyed, there's no telling what her new role, if at all, would be.

She looked down at her clothes. Jeans and a flowing black lace top. Try as she might, she could not remember this particular style. Strange. However, right now it was not a priority.

And so, she closed her eyes and grimaced, and pulled herself to her feet. She wobbled a little bit. So far, so good. That was the good news. The bad news was the beeping inside her head became more insistent.

She may not have been awake for very long, but she had been alive long enough to know that that meant the possible destruction of the space station was imminent.

Ten seconds later, she was sprinting down the hallway. Space station residents would whisper and hug the walls at her approach. She didn't even have to ask them to move. Something was different, very different than the last time she was awakened. Something that she couldn't put her finger on, but it would have to wait.

~

Scythe turned his attention now to MACRO, who was beeping furiously at the orb.

"One, one, one..."

The initial adrenaline shock of the countdown had worn off, but the danger was obviously still there. There was no way she was going to stand there and let that monster stop MACRO from diffusing the bomb. Lyra had only one play. She rushed Scythe with a primal scream. *You want me? Well, here I come.*

She only got within ten feet of Scythe when he made eye contact with her through the mask and reached out to her with a hand.

Something loud and overpowering hit her mind. That's what it felt like. Like somebody had taken a frying pan and hit her in the brain with it, bypassing the rest of her body.

Lyra dropped to her knees. She felt the sensation of her knees hitting the waiting area floor. Then everything went white.

Lyra had never lost consciousness before, but she expected everything to turn black, not white. After the initial blast of color or lack thereof, she regained some semblance of her vision. Only now it was different. The saturation was off or something. She looked around at everybody fighting, and the way she was processing everything, it seemed like a slow motion out of body experience. And that's when she looked down and saw her actual body, unconscious on the floor.

Everybody in the room looked different in the light of this new reality, but Scythe was completely transformed. Instead of weird rotting face and stiff movements, he was tall, muscular, and beautiful. She shook her head. In this reality, he looked like a superhero. Whatever was going on, she didn't like it, and alarm bells were going off in a far corner of her brain. There just wasn't anything she could do about it.

Scythe turned his attention and his face toward her while simultaneously pivoting and battling several opponents at the same time. None of this was making sense to her anymore. He gave her a smile and a nod. She heard his voice inside her head.

"Welcome, Lyra. You will be happy here."

The voice sent a tingling of happiness, peace, and well-being down to her core. She was overcome with the overwhelming happiness, but at the same time she could feel a tiny piece of herself screaming. The tiny piece of her that seemed to be objecting was getting farther and farther away.

Another glance showed that patient zero had also transformed. Instead of a balding, middle aged freak with liquid oozing from his eyes, he was young and strong and fierce. He waved at her too.

Lyra watched Arthur take several blows from the patient and curl into a ball. Grayson was doing his best, kicking a rat and throwing a ceramic mug at Scythe, who dodged it easily. Ian looked down at Lyra's physical body and screamed, reaching out to pick up his disrupter weapon again.

Something caught her eye, a crackle of light, something with possibly a tinge of blue. It streaked across the room and then dissolved. Whatever it was, it caused her to cringe and shrink back in fear. She had no idea why, but she noticed that Scythe also seemed afraid of it. Whatever was going on now, Lyra knew she was on the wrong team.

A little voice in the back of her mind was screaming a name over and over again.

MACRO. Oh yeah, the robot. Lyra hovered over toward the welcome desk and there he was. Lyra was astonished. Instead of the small, dented, obsolete robot with the blue fin on his head, she saw what looked like a super processor on wheels. MACRO was working so hard at his calculations that smoke was literally coming out of his ears as he stared at the small orb, which had transformed into a symbol for four sticks of dynamite.

A crackle rippled across Lyra's mind, coming out of nowhere. She felt herself being ripped backward and down. She felt herself hit the floor again, and yet somehow the sensation of physical feeling was strange and unreal. Then, everything really did go black.

23

Grayson watched Lyra rush Scythe, and then he watched her go down. "No!" Grayson yelled. "What are you doing to her?"

He watched Ian's disrupter swerve over toward Scythe, but with a wave of his hand, Scythe sent him flying. Ian's improvised weapon skittered across the floor.

Then Scythe sent Vax and Maura flying as well, freeing up several unskewered zombie rats. Arthur was still grappling with the slow, but surprisingly tenacious zombie patient. The intermittent sound of the operating saw just added to the horror noise cacophony in the room.

The only thing for certain was the fact that he was in charge. And whether they were all about to die or not, he was tired of being ignored.

"All right, everybody!" he screamed loud enough that every head in the room turned to him, including Scythe. And yes, it had fully occurred to him that the effort was going to get him killed, but at least he would go out in charge, sort of, with everybody in the room finally paying attention to him.

That's when behind him, the door went flying off the hinges. He turned to see a tall, spindly, cyber Morticia enter the room. Her face was jagged, her clothes were ancient, and her expression was grave.

"What the-"

"Interloper!" Cyborg Morticia screamed, and Grayson could swear that iron veins were visible in her gaunt neck. "You will leave now, or I will take you apart molecule by molecule."

Grayson's gaze swung over to Scythe. Scythe repositioned his hands to deal with the new threat and released Lyra. In fact, Grayson could swear that he saw fear ripple across Scythe's mask.

Lyra tried and failed to get to her feet. Grayson rushed over to her and caught her, backing up and pulling her out of the way.

"Everybody out!" Grayson pointed to the opening where the jammed door used to be and yelled loud enough for the space station residents to hear, but hopefully not loud enough to distract the two newly feuding freaks. He grabbed a weapon on the floor and backed up with Lyra to a wall where he could take care of her.

Crash looked up and made eye contact for a moment before retreating to the opposite wall supposedly for the purpose of covering the evacuation. He was also closest to MACRO and the orb. Barely audible above everything else was the continuing nearly final countdown. "One, one, one, one..."

It stopped. The bomb stopped its countdown. Grayson closed his eyes in case that meant it was going off. Then he opened them again. *The little robot did it!*

People were still streaming out of the door and soon it was just him, Crash, and Lyra left in the battle.

Lyra stirred and looked around. "Callista?"

~

"What's going on, Grayson?" Lyra asked, her words slurring. Her body was trembling. She tried to crawl further away, but she was having trouble coordinating her movements.

"Um," Grayson said. "Let's see, the little robot diffused the bomb and Vax took care of most of the rats. Then this one came flying in here out of nowhere," he pointed at Callista, "busting the door down to fight that one." He pointed at Scythe.

"That's Callista," Lyra said weakly. "The cyborg looking Morticia one, not the evil mad scientist one. I thought you had seen her before."

"No," Grayson answered. "I'd remember. You think you can move? I'd like to get out of here, bomb or no bomb."

Lyra couldn't look away though. Both of the figures were doing some weird sort of psychic battle with each other and using ancient and super-lame verbal jabs. Their faces were contorted in concentration and their hands were flailing around with imaginary blows.

But Lyra had been inside the mad scientist's head, or maybe it was the other way around. The whole thing was kind of fuzzy. Maybe there was something from her experience that could help.

She tried to think back at the entire experience. She was shaken at how positive it had been, how beautiful, and how even now, even knowing what she knew, she had an intense desire to go back.

She shuddered. A shame washed over her at not being able to control her emotions. Then she remembered, the one that she had feared on the inside, maybe it was the one thing that Scythe feared too. She took a very deep breath, fighting the idea that she was about to betray the closest, most intimate friend she had ever had. Why was this so hard? *Focus, Lyra.*

"Callista, hit him with the color blue!" She didn't even know if it would matter, but it was all she had. Callista, for her part, adjusted her stance and switched hands. The two of them then exchanged what looked and sounded like a series of lightning bolts.

Grayson started dragging Lyra out the door. Ian darted in and helped, and they made it around the corner. They could still hear the fireworks, but for now they were in the clear.

After a few minutes, there was a loud scream and then everything went silent. The sound of footsteps crunching through the rubble rang out. The space station residents cringed waiting to see who would emerge.

It was Callista, clothes all askew. She stomped toward them, stopping for a very brief moment to smooth the jagged hair on her head. "Lyra," she said and nodded, and then continued walking slowly down the hallway and out of sight. They all continued watching in the direction that she had disappeared. Then a few brave souls peeked inside the waiting area.

What they said they found inside was substantial cosmetic damage to the room, a happy and intact MACRO, and Crash and Merck happily dispatching the last of the mutant rats.

"Where did Scythe go?" Lyra asked Crash later.

"I have no idea," he had said, "he literally disappeared in front of my eyes, clothes and all."

Lyra wondered if Callista had made good on her promise to take the scientist apart at the molecular level and wondered if that was even possible.

As they all sat in the hallway outside of the demolished waiting room, she quizzed Crash over and over on his eyewitness account of what he had seen and heard while she was unconscious and after Grayson dragged her to safety.

Mostly it was because, deep down somewhere she hadn't known existed before that day, something was awake. And somehow, that part of her knew that Scythe was still alive and out there somewhere, a thought that brought both horror and hope to her soul in a dichotomy that would haunt her dreams.

"Hey Grayson," Vax said at last. "It turns out that your daytime show guess about the patient was totally right. It was an AI Zombie."

The hallway roared with the sound of laughter.

That's when a vivid blue, goth Cecaelia came swishing down the hallway out of nowhere.

"Please tell me that somebody else sees her," Lyra said out loud, starting to suspect that she could add a concussion to her list of possible injuries. Then she remembered having seen her the other night at Chez Vray.

"Hello," the blue apparition with the sparkly tentacles said. "You guys haven't seen a weird guy in a Halloween mask come through here have you? Because I'm going to ring his scrawny little neck until his eyeballs pop out-"

She stopped as it just then occurred to her that something had happened here and that they were all paying more attention to her than she expected.

"Oh please," she continued, with a flourish of tentacle. "This jackass propositioned my client, saying he'd free him or something. Well, I know a two-bit huckster when I hear about one and if you ask me, he deserves whatever he gets. You guys are with me, right? Plus, I hear that security on this space station is nearly nonexistent."

"Hey," Crash objected. "I'm all the security this space station will ever need."

"Sure, sure," she said, looking down at him as he sat in the hallway. "Good for you, you keep trying."

"You just missed him," Lyra said. "He's gone."

The blue goth apparition came over to Lyra. "Hello, my name is Astrid, and you are?" She held out a tentacle, which Lyra happily shook.

Lyra found herself in a very punchy mood. Being surprised at still being alive will do that, apparently.

"Lyra. And I like your shiny tentacles."

Astrid frowned. "You people look awful. What the hell

happened here?"

"Halloween mask guy," Lyra answered. "Did all of that. Well most of it, we helped a little." She pointed inside at the waiting room.

Astrid peeked her head in there and made a whistling sound. "Wow, that place is going to need a lot of work. Probably for the best. First thing I'd do is get rid of that lime Koolaid paint."

"Hey!" Gorb objected.

Astrid went back over to Lyra and kneeled. "Now when you say this guy is gone, do you mean I missed him by ten minutes and he went that way gone?" She pointed down the hall. "Or transported out of here gone or somebody shot him and he's dead gone?"

"Crash?" Lyra asked. Since he was the one who had seen it all go down, she figured he was the best one to answer.

"Lightning, star-wars, death battle where he vanished in front of my eyes clothes and all gone," Crash answered.

Lyra nodded.

"Well, then," Astrid said thoughtfully to Lyra. "Guess that's that. Here's my card, dearie, you look like you might need it."

A shiny business card appeared in her hand and she handed it to Lyra, who read it aloud. *Astrid, short-term magic for real-world problems.*

"Cool," Lyra said, but then the card vanished. "Hey! Where did it go?"

"It integrated my contact info into your cellphone, dearie. Get with the times, would you? Adorable robot by the way. I'm sure I'll be seeing you people later."

She turned her attention to Ian. "Hey, you look familiar, aren't you that fear guy? From the web show?"

"Oh yeah," said Nancy, snapping her finger, "that's where I know him from. Lyra, you've been holding out on us."

"Knew it," said Astrid. "I never forget a face." And with that she left,

snaking a tentacle around Arthur's wrist as she went by. Lyra could have sworn she muttered. "Don't knock it until you've tried it, big boy."

~

Lyra entered the waiting room with Arthur. "Hi, Gorb!"

"Hi Lyra," he answered, shimmying even more than usual. He had his radio turned up and a cup of fresh, steaming coffee at his desk. "No crazy singing patients or rat bites today."

"Thank goodness for that," she answered. "Unlike you, I like being bored. At least a little."

Arthur came in the room. "Morning, Lyra. Good news."

"Yeah?" Lyra asked.

"The rat bite victim, Steve, is conscious and almost back to normal. The increased brain activity eventually subsided, in much the same way as a case of inflammation."

"That is good news," Lyra said. "I'm sure you won't be missing any of our weird scientist invasions or mutant rat infestations when you're gone. I heard you got a cushy job back in the Omega system. Congratulations."

"Well, they offered, but I turned them down."

Lyra turned to him. "What?"

"I think I'll stay here for a while."

"Glad to hear it." Lyra smiled at him. Her phone made a notification sound. She glanced down. The message was from Ian.

"Oh," Gorb said, "going on another date tonight, I see."

"Gorb, stop snooping! And it isn't a date, exactly. Ian has volunteered to stay on the station for a while and set up an electronic perimeter using the disrupter that worked on Scythe. Hopefully that will keep him away."

"What'll keep him away is the fact that he's probably dead." Grayson practically materialized out of nowhere.

Lyra wished people would stop doing that to her. Lyra smiled at him. Then she leaned forward and gave him a kiss on the cheek. "Thanks for saving me, you old goat."

His face turned red and he wandered off. Lyra just smiled, and swiped Gorb's coffee again.

"Hey!" Gorb objected.

Just another day on Celestica.

ABOUT THE AUTHOR

L.A. Johnson writes fun, original Sci-Fi you won't find anywhere else.

Leave a Review for this book on Amazon

Connect with me
www.lajbooks.com

Made in United States
North Haven, CT
10 August 2024

55899710R00114